'Coffee? Lunch? I don't know— just the chance to catch up.'

Her heart hitched against her ribs. She wasn't sure she wanted to catch up. She'd worked so hard to put Sam behind her, and she'd battened down her heart around her memories of Jack. 'Catching up' sounded like the perfect way of ripping it all open again, exposing the wound and prodding it just for the hell of it.

'I don't know,' she said honestly, not wanting to hurt him, but not willing to hurt herself again either. 'I'm not sure I want to, Sam. It was a long time ago—a lot of water under the bridge.'

His face became shuttered, and she could feel him withdrawing, all that glorious warmth pulling away from her and leaving her cold and lonely and aching.

Caroline Anderson has the mind of a butterfly. She's been a nurse, a secretary, a teacher, run her own soft-furnishing business and now she's settled on writing. She says, 'I was looking for that elusive something. I finally realised it was variety, and now I have it in abundance. Every book brings new horizons and new friends, and in between books I have learned to be a juggler. My teacher husband John and I have two beautiful and talented daughters, Sarah and Hannah, umpteen pets and several acres of Suffolk that nature tries to reclaim every time we turn our backs!' Caroline also writes for the Mills & Boon® Tender Romance™ series.

Recent titles by the same author:

ASSIGNMENT: SINGLE MAN—
  Double Destiny duo (Tender Romance™)
ASSIGNMENT: SINGLE FATHER—
  Double Destiny duo (Medical Romance™)
ACCIDENTAL SEDUCTION
A VERY SINGLE WOMAN

THE BABY BONDING

BY
CAROLINE ANDERSON

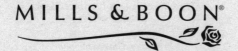

MILLS & BOON®

First published in Great Britain 2003
Harlequin Mills & Boon Limited,
Eton House, 18-24 Paradise Road, Richmond, Surrey TW9 1SR

© Caroline Anderson 2003

ISBN 0 263 83472 7

Set in Times Roman 10½ on 12¼ pt.
03-1003-49567

Printed and bound in Spain
by Litografía Rosés, S.A., Barcelona

CHAPTER ONE

IT COULDN'T be him.

Not now, surely, when she'd got over him at last, stopped thinking about him every minute of the day, finally stopped caring if he was alive or dead.

No. She hadn't stopped caring. She'd never stop caring about that, but she'd stopped obsessing about it.

More or less.

And now here he was in front of her, as large as life and handsome as the devil, his face creased with laughter as always, and the sound of his deep chuckle sent shivers running through her. His long, rangy body was propped up against a pillar by the desk, and his pale blue theatre scrubs hung on his frame.

He'd lost weight, she thought with shock. He'd never been heavy, but now he was lean, and amongst the laughter lines there were others that hadn't been there before. Deeper ones that owed nothing to humour.

He's older, she reminded herself—three years. He must be nearly thirty-five. He was a little less than two years older than her, and she'd be thirty-three soon. How time passed. Gracious, she'd only been twenty-eight when they'd met, thirty the year Jack had been born.

Jack.

She swallowed the lump. Some things you never got over.

He shrugged away from the pillar and turned towards her, and for a moment he froze.

Then an incredulous smile split his face and he strode

down the ward towards her, arms outstretched, and she found herself wrapped hard against the solid warmth of his chest.

'Molly!'

The word was muffled in her hair, but after a second he released her, grasping her shoulders in his big, strong hands and holding her at arm's length, studying her with those amazing blue eyes.

'My God, it really is you!' he exclaimed, and hugged her again, then stood back once more as if he couldn't quite believe his eyes.

Her defences trashed by the spontaneous warmth of his welcome, she smiled up at him. 'Hello, Sam,' she said softly. She could hardly hear her voice over the pounding of her heart, and she felt her smile falter with the strength of her tumbling emotions. She pulled herself together with an effort. 'How are you?'

So polite, so formal, but then they always had been, really. It had been that sort of relationship, of necessity.

His mouth kicked up in a crooked grin that didn't quite reach his eyes, and her heart stuttered for a second. Was something wrong? Something with Jack?

'OK, I suppose,' he said lightly. Too lightly. Something *was* wrong. 'Busy,' he added, 'but, then, I'm always busy. Goes with the territory.'

'And—Jack?' she asked, hardly daring to say the words.

The grin softened, his eyes mellowing, and she felt the tension ease.

'Jack's great,' he said. 'He's at school now. Well, nursery, really. He's not old enough for school yet. And you? How are you? And why are you here?'

She smiled a little unsteadily, the relief making her light-headed. 'I work here—I'm a midwife, remember?'

He looked at her then, registering her uniform as if for

the first time, and a puzzled frown pleated his brow. 'I thought you worked as a community midwife?'

'I did, but not now. I only ever wanted to work part time, and it's easier to do that in a hospital, so when this job came up, I applied for it. But what about you? I didn't know you worked here—how did you keep that a secret?'

He laughed, his eyes crinkling again. 'No secret. I wasn't here until a few days ago, and I had no idea you were here, either. You used to live the other side of Ipswich, so you must have moved, too, unless you're commuting.'

'No, I'm not commuting, we've moved. We live in Audley now—near Mick's parents, so they can see Libby. I've been working here for six months.'

He shook his head, his eyes bemused. 'Amazing—but I suppose I shouldn't be surprised. There aren't that many hospitals, and it's not the first time I've run into someone I know.' He glanced up and checked the clock on the wall. 'Look—are you busy now?'

She gave a tired laugh. 'I'm always busy—it goes with the territory,' she said, quoting his words back at him. 'What did you have in mind?'

'Coffee? Lunch? I don't know—just a chance to catch up.'

Her heart hitched against her ribs. She wasn't sure she wanted to catch up. She'd worked so hard to put Sam and Crystal behind her, and she'd battened down her heart around her memories of Jack. 'Catching up' sounded like the perfect way of ripping it all open again, exposing the wound and prodding it just for the hell of it.

'I don't know,' she said honestly, not wanting to hurt him, but not willing to hurt herself again, either. 'I'm not sure I want to, Sam. It was a long time ago—a lot of water under the bridge.'

His face became shuttered, and she could feel him withdrawing, all that glorious warmth pulling away from her and leaving her cold and lonely and aching.

'Of course. I'm sorry, I didn't mean to be so thoughtless. Well, it's lovely to see you looking so well. No doubt I'll see you again.'

And turning on his heel, he strode away, leaving her standing there in a daze.

Idiot, she chastised herself. You fool! You should have talked to him. You're going to have to work together, how can it help you to have this cold and awkward distance between you? And there's Jack...

Jack's not your son, she told herself. Let it go.

She dragged in a deep breath and stared blindly out of the window. Count to ten, she told herself. Or twenty.

Or ten zillion.

Or you could just go after him.

She went, freeing her feet from the floor with a superhuman effort and then, once she'd started to move, almost running after him down the corridor.

She reached the lobby just as the lift doors were sliding shut, and called his name.

A hand came out, blocking the doors, and they hissed open and he stepped out, his expression still guarded.

He didn't say anything, just stood there waiting, watching her. The lift doors slid shut again behind him, but still he stood there. Oh, lord. She looked down, unsure what to say, then abandoned subterfuge and pretence. She'd never been any good at it, anyway. She let her breath go on a little whoosh.

'I'm sorry,' she said softly. 'I didn't mean to sound so cold. I'd love to have coffee with you.'

He was silent for a second, then nodded slowly. 'Now? Or later?'

She shrugged. 'Now would be fine for me. I was going to take a break now anyway, and nobody's doing anything exciting at the moment. If things change they'll page me. How about you?'

'I'm fine. I've finished in Theatre. I only had a short list this morning, and we're all done. I was just going to change and do a bit of admin. You'll be doing me a huge favour if you take me away from it.'

She laughed, as she was meant to, and, instead of calling the lift again, he ushered her towards the stairs. They went down to the little coffee-shop at the back of the hospital, the one, she told him, that members of the public hadn't really discovered, and he bought them coffee and sticky gingerbread slices and carried them over to a sofa. It was by the window, tucked in a corner overlooking a courtyard, and it was the closest thing they'd get to privacy.

For a moment neither of them said anything, and Molly wondered what on earth she was doing here with him. She must be mad.

He'd leant forward, his elbows on his knees, his fingers interlinked and apparently requiring his full attention, and she wondered what he was thinking. Then he looked across at her, catching her with her guard down, and his eyes seemed to spear right through to her soul.

'So—how are you?' he said, his voice low. 'Honestly?'

She shrugged, suddenly swallowing tears. 'I'm all right. Still the merry widow.' Her laugh was hollow and humourless, and he searched her face with those piercing blue eyes that missed nothing.

'Ah, Molly,' he said gruffly, and, reaching out, he gave her fingers a quick squeeze. 'I had hoped you'd be married again by now, settled down with someone worthy of your love.'

'I am with someone. I've got Libby.'

'A man, I meant.'

'We don't all need to be in a relationship, Sam,' she pointed out softly. 'Sometimes it's better not to be.'

She looked away, not wanting him to read her eyes, but he was looking down at his hands again anyway, staring fixedly at his fingers as they threaded and unthreaded through each other. When he spoke, his voice was gruff.

'I'm sorry I reacted like that—assuming you'd be as pleased to see me as I am to see you. It was crass of me. I apologise. I should have realised you'd moved on.'

'I *am* pleased to see you,' she told him, unable to lie, unable to let him believe anything less than the truth. 'It's just—I found it so hard, three years ago. I didn't think I would, but it's been really difficult, and I didn't want to stir it all up, but now it is, anyway, and—well, I've longed to know how he is.'

He looked up and she met his eyes, and she saw sorrow and compassion in them, and an amazing tenderness. 'He's wonderful, Molly. Beautiful. Jack's the best thing that's ever happened to me. He's brought me more joy than I could ever have imagined—and I owe it all to you.'

She swallowed again, shocked at how readily the tears seemed to form. She was always so grounded, so sensible, so dispassionate.

But not about Jack.

'I'd love to see a photo,' she said, wondering if she was just opening herself up to heartache but unable to deny herself this one small thing.

'A photo?' He laughed softly. 'I've got hundreds—and videos going back to his birth. You're welcome to them. Why don't you come round? Then you can meet him, too.'

An ache so large it threatened to destroy her built in her chest. 'But Crystal didn't want us to stay in contact.'

'And I never did agree with her. Besides, it's irrelevant,'

he added, his voice curiously flat. 'Crystal's dead, Molly. She died two years ago.'

Molly felt shock drain the blood from her face. 'Dead?' she echoed silently. 'Oh, dear God, Sam, I'm so sorry.'

His face tightened. 'It was a long time ago,' he said, but she could feel his pain, could remember her own when Mick had died, and she ached for him.

She reached out, her hand covering those interlinked fingers, and he turned his hands and caught hers between them, renewing the bond that had been forged three years ago in blood and sweat and tears.

'So—how do you manage?' she asked, her voice surprisingly steady. 'About Jack, I mean? Who looks after him?' Oh, lord, she thought, tell me you're not married again. Tell me someone else isn't bringing him up.

'I have a couple who live in the house—Mark's disabled after an accident and can only do very light work, and Debbie needs to be around to look after him, but between them they look after the house and the garden and take Jack to and from nursery. They do it in return for their accommodation and a small salary, and because they live on the premises it gives me cover when I'm on call for the night or the weekend or whatever, and it's much better than having an au pair. Been there, done that, and this is streets better.'

'Gosh. You were lucky to find them. Do you think they'll be all right? Does Jack like them, or is it too soon to tell?'

He smiled. 'Jack loves them and, yes, I was lucky, but it's not a new arrangement. They've been with me for a year now, and so far it's been brilliant. Mark's a tapestry designer—he's a great big guy, an ex-biker with multiple piercings and the most unlikely looking person with a needle and thread, but he's amazingly gifted, really successful, and Debbie's just a miniature powerhouse. She makes me tired just watching her.'

'Didn't they mind moving up from London?'

'Didn't seem to, but it's early days. We only moved three weeks ago, and I've only been in this job three days.'

While she'd been on her days off, of course, which was why she hadn't known he was here.

A pity. It might have given her a chance to prepare.

Or run.

His bleeper summoned him and, standing up, he drained his coffee and shot her an apologetic smile.

'Later—we'll talk some more. Perhaps over dinner.'

She smiled and gave a noncommittal nod. 'Perhaps,' she said silently to his retreating back, and wondered what hand fate, with her twisted sense of humour, would deal them this time.

It wasn't too late to run...

So many memories.

Crystal, determined and focused, her gimlet mind fastened on this one idea to the exclusion of all others, one last attempt to rescue the tatters of their marriage.

'I want a child,' she'd said. 'What about a surrogate mother? You're in the business—can't you find one?'

And then he had, by a miracle, by sheer coincidence, because a patient of his had had a baby for someone else, and he'd talked to her, told her about Crystal's idea.

'You need to talk to my friend Molly,' she'd said, and then Molly had been there, coming through the door behind him, warm and generous and full of life and laughter, filling the room with sunshine and making him glad to be alive. His first impression of her had been that he'd could trust her with his life and with that of his child, and nothing she'd ever done had taken that away.

They'd become friends over the next few weeks and months, and she'd been a rock during the endless procedures, the meetings, the conversations, the dealings with the solicitors. He remembered how calm she'd been, how in control, how understanding and gentle with Crystal.

The pregnancy had seemed to last for ever, such a long wait until the phone call came to say she was in labour, and he could remember every moment of the drive to the hospital, the waiting again, and then being there, holding Molly, supporting her while she'd given birth to Jack— the son he and Crystal had thought they'd never have.

Their son, carried for them by Molly, who'd generously agreed to act as a host mother to their embryo. A tummy mummy, she'd called herself, and their son had been loved and nurtured and protected by her body until the time had been right to hand him over to them.

And then Jack—tiny, screaming, enraged by the insult of birth, only calming when the midwife had taken him from the panic-striken Crystal and given him to Sam.

Then Molly had let out a long, ragged breath and smiled tearfully at him and nodded, and it had been all right.

Or so he'd thought, for the last three years.

And now he'd seen her again, and she'd admitted she'd had problems, and the doubts had come back to plague him. Had it been the right thing to do, to ask another woman to make such stupendous sacrifices for them, so Crystal could have what she wanted?

He nearly laughed out loud. What she'd *thought* she wanted, anyway. What was that saying? Be careful what you wish for, you might get it?

'So—is it possible?'

Matt Jordan, the A and E consultant, stood beside Sam with his hands thrust into the pockets of his white coat, watching as he examined their patient. It was the first time he'd met the big Canadian, and he liked him instinctively—not least for calling him so quickly on this somewhat puzzling case.

'She could be pregnant, yes. Certainly looks possible.' Sam gently palpated the distended abdomen of the unconscious woman in Resus and shook his head thoughtfully. 'I think you're right, I think she is pregnant, but I can't be sure without a scan or a pregnancy test. It could be all sorts of things—a tumour, an ovarian cyst, fibroids—without a heartbeat it's anybody's guess, and I can't pick one up on the foetal stethoscope. It could just be fluid, but it doesn't really feel right for that. What do you know about her?' he asked Matt.

'Very little,' he was told. 'She was brought in a few minutes ago after collapsing at the wheel of her car. The police are working on it, but it doesn't seem to be registered to a woman, so they don't know who she is. They're checking with the car's owner.'

He nodded.

'Well, the first thing we need is an ultrasound to check if there's a live baby, and we'll go from there. In the meantime do nothing that would compromise the baby if you can avoid it. Once we know if she's carrying a live foetus, we can get a proper scan to work out its gestational age and decide if it's viable if we need to do an emergency section for any reason. I don't suppose you can hazard a guess as to what's wrong with her?'

'No. Not diabetes, we've checked that, and her heart seems fine. Pupils are a bit iffy, so it could be drugs or a bang on the head. Could it be anything obstetric?'

Sam frowned and shook his head. 'Don't think so. It's hard to tell without more information. I want that scan, fast. If she's twenty-eight weeks or more and remains stable and unconscious, we can remove the baby to give her more chance, if necessary, but the baby's chances will decrease with every week less than that. And, of course, there are other complications. She's a smoker, for a start, so it might be small for dates, and starting from a disadvantage. Still, there's no point in speculating till we get the scan and know if she is pregnant and the baby's still alive. If she is pregnant, we'll take her down to the big scanner and have a better look if you think she's stable enough.'

The young nurse beside him frowned in puzzlement. 'How do you know she's a smoker?'

He shrugged. 'She smells of smoke—and her teeth are stained.'

His eyes met Matt's. 'She's a heavy smoker, I'd say, so watch her lungs, too, with the added stress of pregnancy. She might have breathing difficulties—and if she shows signs of respiratory distress or hypovolaemia, call me. She might get an amniotic fluid embolus or an antepartum haemorrhage as a result of the impact.'

'We'll watch for that. She's got a wedge under her left hip to take the pressure off her aorta and vena cava. Anything else specific we should be doing?'

He shook his head. 'Not really. Some answers would be good. Bleep me again if you need me, and when you get the results of the ultrasound. I'll be in my office.'

Sam walked back up there, unable to do any more without further information, and at the moment at least she seemed stable. He'd worry about her once he knew a little more but, in the meantime, other thoughts were clamouring for his attention.

With each step, the young woman faded further from his mind, crowded out by an image of Molly that blanked his thoughts to anything else.

She hadn't changed at all—well, not enough to notice. She'd got her pre-pregnancy figure back, of course, but apart from that she seemed no different. Her eyes were still that same warm, gentle shade of brown, her hair a few tones darker and shot through with gold, and her smile...

He felt choked, just thinking about her smile. She smiled with her whole face, not just that gorgeous, mobile mouth that was so amazingly expressive.

He growled under his breath. So she was an attractive woman. So what? So were lots of women. Hell, he worked with young, attractive women all day, both staff and patients, and he managed to cope. So why had he picked on Molly, of all people, to be so acutely aware of? She was the last woman in the world he could entertain those sorts of thoughts about.

His relationship with her was hugely complex because of Jack, and absolutely the last thing it needed was any further layers added to it!

'Keep breathing, nice light breaths—that's it, that's lovely. You're doing really well.'

Liz, her young patient, sobbed and shook her head. 'I can't do this...'

'Yes, you can,' Molly told her calmly, recognising her panic for what it was, a sign that she was moving into the transitional phase between the first and second stages of labour. 'You'll be fine.'

'I bet you've never had any babies, midwives never have,' she said with no real venom.

Molly gave a soft laugh. 'Sorry—I've had three.'

'You're mad. I'm never having another,' the girl moaned, leaning against her partner and biting her lip. 'God, I hate you! How could you do this to me, you bastard? I never want to speak to you again.'

He met Molly's eyes over her shoulder, panic flaring in

them, and she squeezed his hand as it lay on the girl's shoulder and smiled reassuringly at him.

'She's getting closer. Tempers often fray and it's usually the father who gets it. She'll be fine.'

'Going to be sick,' Liz said, and promptly was, all down his front.

To his credit he didn't even wince, just led her back to the bed and wiped her mouth, then looked at Molly. 'I could do with cleaning up,' he said softly, and she nodded.

'We'll get you some theatre pyjamas to wear. Just sit with her for a second.'

She slipped out, grabbed the scrubs from the linen store and was about to mop up when Liz's waters broke.

'OK, let's get you back on the bed and check you. I reckon it'll soon be over now,' she said encouragingly. When she examined her patient, though, she found that the cord had prolapsed down beside the baby's head, and when she checked the foetal heart rate, it was dipping alarmingly.

It would be over soon, but not for the reason she'd thought!

'Liz, I want you to turn on your side for me,' she said, pressing the crash button by the head of the bed and dropping the backrest simultaneously. 'We've got a bit of a problem with the baby's cord, and I want to get your head down and hips up a bit, to take the pressure off. It's nothing to worry about, but we need to move fast, and I'm going to get some help.'

'Need a hand here?'

Sam's deep, reassuring voice was the most wonderful sound in Molly's world at that moment.

'Prolapsed cord,' she said quietly. 'Her waters went a moment ago, and she had quite a lot of fluid. Watch where you walk, by the way. Liz, this is Mr Gregory.'

'Hello, Liz,' he said, moving in beside her and throwing her a quick, reassuring smile before he lifted her hips effortlessly and slid a pillow under them. He met Molly's eyes. 'What's the previous history?'

She shook her head. 'None. First baby, full term—'

'And the last,' Liz groaned. 'What's happening?'

'The cord's got squashed between your cervix and the baby's head,' Sam told her calmly. 'We've got a choice under these conditions. We can deliver the baby as quickly as possible the normal way, with the help of forceps, or give you a Caesarian section. I just need to take a quick look at you to help me decide which is the best option, OK? Gloves, Molly.'

She handed him the box, and he snapped them on and quickly checked the baby's presentation and the extent of the prolapse of the cord. As he straightened, he met Molly's eyes again, his own unreadable. 'What do you think?' he asked. 'Want to try?'

She shrugged, not wanting to argue with him on their first shared case, but deeply concerned because it was a first baby and it was still a little high for comfort. If she had problems...

'We can try, I suppose, if you want to—but we haven't got long.'

He nodded agreement, and approval flickered in his eyes. 'I know. Let's go for a section. Push that head back, Molly, until the cord's pulsating again, and hold it there until she's in Theatre. I don't think we can get the cord back up, there's too big a loop, so we just have to keep the pressure off. I'm going to scrub.'

The room had been filling up while they talked, people responding to the crash call, and he turned to his SHO. 'Get a line in, please, and give her oxygen, and terbutaline to slow the contractions if we can. Cross-match for two units as well, please. I'll see you in Theatre, Liz. Don't worry, we'll soon have your baby out.'

He squeezed her partner's shoulder on the way out, and Molly thought how like him that was, sparing a thought for the shocked young man standing paralysed on the sidelines, even in such a chaotic moment. He'd always seemed to have time for things others often overlooked.

Within a very few minutes Liz was on her way to Theatre, Molly's gloved hand firmly pushing the baby's head back away from her cervix, keeping the pressure off the cord to prevent the baby dying from lack of oxygen.

They didn't have much time, but as long as she could keep that cord pulsating, the baby stood a good chance of coming through this unharmed.

Sam was waiting, and he wasted no time in opening Liz up once she was under the anaesthetic. Her partner, David, was hovering outside Theatre and had looked scared to death, but Molly didn't really have time to worry about him.

All her attention was on holding that baby's head back, during the shift across to the operating table, positioning Liz ready for surgery with the head of the table tilted downwards, and trying desperately to ignore the cramp in her arm and back from the awkward position she was in.

Finally she felt the pressure ease, and looked up to meet Sam's eyes as he lifted the baby clear and handed it to the waiting nurse.

'It's a boy,' he told Molly, throwing a quick smile in her direction before returning his attention to Liz. 'Time of birth fifteen twenty-seven. He's all yours, Molly.'

She straightened and flexed her shoulders, then, after clamping and cutting the cord, she took the baby immediately over to the waiting crib and sucked out his airways. His cry, weak and intermittent until that point, changed pitch with indignation and turned into a full-blown bellow, and she felt the tension in the room ease.

'Apgar score nine at one minute,' she said, and glanced up at the clock on the wall. She'd check again at fifteen thirty-two, by which time she was sure the slight blueness of his skin would have gone and he would score a perfect ten.

Relief made her almost light-headed, and she smiled down at the screaming baby, his colour improving and turning pink as she watched. His heartbeat was strong, his cry once he'd got going was good and loud, and his muscle tone and response to suction had been excellent.

It was a pity things had gone wrong so Liz had missed his birth, she thought, wrapping him up in heated towels and taking him out of the Theatre to David, but trying for a normal delivery would have been too risky. She'd known doctors who would have taken the risk, others who would have gone for the section without a second thought regardless of the circumstances.

Sam, thank God, didn't seem to fall into either of those categories. He'd rapidly weighed up both options in the light of his examination, and had made what she felt had been the right decision. She felt able to trust his judgement—and that was a relief, as she was going to have to work with him.

She pictured his eyes again over the mask when he'd smiled, his eyes crinkling at the corners. She'd always loved that about him, the way he smiled with his eyes...

'Is everything all right?' David asked, and she nodded, putting the baby in his slightly tense arms.

'So far, so good. I've done a quick check and all the obvious bits are present and correct, and Liz is doing really well.' She smiled up at David, but he didn't notice. He was staring down in frank amazement at his son.

'We've got a baby,' he said, his voice faintly incredulous. Lifting his free hand, he stroked one finger gently down the baby's translucent, downy cheek, still streaked with blood and vernix. The little head turned towards the finger, his rosebud mouth pursing, and Molly smiled, an all-too-familiar lump in her throat.

'He's hungry. She can feed him just as soon as she comes round, but in the meantime he just needs a cuddle from his dad. Just hold him and talk to him for a minute. He'd recognise your voice, he will have heard it from the womb. He's a bit messy, but we won't wash him until Liz has woken up and seen him, or it could be anybody's baby.'

He nodded, and she took him through to Recovery to wait for Liz while she herself went back into Theatre to check on her.

'Apgar up to ten?' Sam asked, checking on the baby's progress even as he worked on Liz.

'Yes—he's fine now. His colour was a bit off, but it's not surprising.'

'You did a good job,' Sam said softly to her, and she felt her skin warm.

'You aren't making too big a fist of it yourself,' she said with a smile, and he chuckled quietly under his breath.

'You're too kind. The placenta's there, by the way.'

She studied it carefully, making sure no parts of it were missing and likely to cause the mother future problems, and nodded. 'It's OK.'

'Good. Now, could you do me a favour, Molly, if you're happy with the baby? Can you phone down to A and E and ask about the young woman who was brought in a couple of hours ago—query pregnant, no ID, unconscious in the car?'

'Sure.'

She used the theatre phone, and discovered that the woman had regained consciousness and discharged herself.

Sam frowned, his brows drawing together in disapproval. 'Did they scan her?'

She shook her head. 'Not that they said. She came round just after you left her, and wouldn't stay another minute. The police think she'd stolen the car, apparently.'

'How bizarre. Oh, well.' He shrugged and carried on with closing Liz while Molly checked the baby again. He was snuggled in his father's arms, blissfully asleep now, and, judging by the look on David's face, he wasn't the only one feeling blissful.

Through the glass she saw Sam straighten up and flex his shoulders. He said something and the anaesthetist nodded, and he stepped back, handing Liz over to the anaesthetic team. Stripping off his gloves and mask, he came out to join them.

'All done, and she's fine. She'll be with us in a minute.' Looking down at the baby, he ran a finger lightly over the back of his tiny hand.

'Hello, little fellow,' he said softly. 'Has he got a name?'

'I don't know. Lucy.'

Sam met David's eyes and smiled. 'That may not be appropriate, under the circumstances.'

David chuckled, his shoulders dropping with the easing of tension. 'Perhaps we'd better think again. I don't know, we were sure she was having a girl. Something about the heartbeat, Liz said. Probably an old wives' tale.' He pulled a face and swallowed hard. 'Um—thanks, by the way. I'm really grateful to you all for getting him out safely. Liz would have been gutted—'

He broke off, and Sam laid a comforting hand on his shoulder.

'Any time,' he said. 'They'll bring her through to Recovery now, and she can hold him and feed him, then Molly will take you all back to the ward once they're happy she's stable. This little fellow seems to be fine, but a paediatrician will come and check him in due course, just as a matter of routine. In the meantime, I'll leave you with Molly. She'll look after you both.'

He threw Molly a smile and went to change, and it was as if the lights had gone out.

Oh, damn. And she'd really, really thought she was over him...

CHAPTER TWO

'HE'S been such a good boy today, haven't you, Jack?'

The little dark head bobbed vigorously, a smile lighting up his face like a beacon. 'I did painting, Daddy—see!'

There was a slightly tattered piece of grey sugar paper held to the fridge door with magnets, and Sam studied the wild, multicoloured handprints on it and felt his heart contract with pride. He grinned a little off-key and ruffled his son's hair.

'So you did. Well done. What else did you do?'

'Um—singing, and played in the sandpit. We had fish fingers for lunch—I'm hungry,' he added, tipping his head back and looking hopefully up at Debbie.

She laughed softly. 'You're always hungry. Come on, sit down at the table and you can have your tea while you tell your dad all about your day, and I'll make him a nice drink. Cuppa, Sam? Mark and I are just having one.'

'Thank you, Debbie, that would be lovely.' He shrugged out of his jacket and glanced across at Debbie's husband. 'Hello, Mark.'

'Hi. You good?'

He smiled tiredly. 'I'll do. Yourself?'

The big man nodded from his seat by the window. 'Good. The latest effort's coming along—what do you think?'

He held up a large square of canvas, and even from across the room Sam could see the wonderfully subtle colours and almost three-dimensional quality of the tapestry Mark was creating. It was a study of leaves, but close up

24

and personal. There was nothing pretty-pretty about it, but there was a vigour in the composition that was the trade mark of all his designs, and this one was no exception.

'You're getting a bit good at this,' Sam said, genuine admiration in his voice, and Mark lifted a shoulder, awkward with the praise.

'I thought I'd do apples and pears next—you know, a sort of orchard theme. Maybe some plums, or autumn leaves. The country's really inspired me—let something loose inside. I just hope they sell.'

'Of course they'll sell. They always sell. The shops love your designs,' Debbie said pragmatically, sliding a mug of tea across the table. 'Sam, take the weight off. You look done in.'

'Busy day,' he said. Busy, and emotionally exhausting. He sat down at the big, scrubbed pine kitchen table that filled the centre of the kitchen and leant back in his chair with a sigh. His mind was whirling with thoughts of Molly, and all he could see was her face. He wished he'd got her number, but he hadn't, so he couldn't ring her—unless she was in the book?

He reached for it, conveniently at arm's length on the dresser behind him, and flicked through the pages. Hammond. There. He ran his finger down the list, and found only a few, none of them Molly.

Unless her initials didn't start with an M. Chewing his lip thoughtfully, he ran his finger down again, and paused. A.M.?

Yes, of course. Annabel Mary, she'd been christened. He remembered now. He remembered a lot of things…

He shut the book. Perhaps he'd ring her later.

But then Jack would be in bed.

Now, then?

He needed to sort out the videos, dig out the photos.

Heaven only knows what's happened to them, he thought. They were probably in the boxes in the loft and they'd take him ages to find.

But Jack was here, now, and Molly's eyes, when he'd talked about the boy…

Picking up his mug, he got up and went into his study and closed the door behind him with a soft click.

Molly stared at the phone warily, hope warring with common sense.

Of course it wouldn't be Sam. He hadn't got her number, unless he'd looked her up in the book, but her first initial wasn't M., so he probably wouldn't find her automatically.

Then again, he'd known her full name all those years ago, seen it enough times on the endless paperwork, so maybe…

'Oh, just answer it,' she muttered to herself, and lifted the receiver. 'Hello?'

'Molly?'

Her heart lurched and steadied again, and she closed her eyes briefly. 'Sam.'

'Hi. I hope you don't mind me ringing. Um, about you seeing Jack—I meant to say something earlier, but I didn't get round to it. Are you busy this evening? I mean, it's not very much notice, but I thought, if you'd like…'

Her heart lurched again, and she threw a quick glance at the door. Libby was on the other side of it, scraping on her violin, trying to get to grips with a difficult passage. She'd done her homework, and now she was grappling with this. She'd been at it for nearly half an hour, but she wouldn't give up until she'd got this bit right, at least. Molly just hoped it was sooner rather than later, for all their sakes.

'What did you have in mind?' she asked cautiously.

'I wondered if you'd like to come over. I mean, don't worry if you've got other plans, or you'd rather not, but I just thought—'

'I haven't got plans,' she said quickly—too quickly. Slow down, she told herself, and drew a deep, steadying breath. 'Tonight would be fine,' she went on, deliberately calming her voice despite the clamouring of her heart. 'I need to check with Libby, of course, but I'm sure there won't be a problem. She'd like to see him, too, I'm sure.'

'Fine. Whenever you're ready—the sooner the better, really, because he goes to bed at about half-seven.'

'That late?' she said, and could have bitten her tongue for the implied criticism. It was none of her business...

'He has a nap when he gets home from nursery, and Debbie lets him sleep as long as he wants. That way I get to see him when I get in,' he told her, and she wasn't sure if she'd imagined a mild note of reproof in his voice. 'Whatever. I think in any case we could make an exception tonight—apart from which, he's as bright as a button to-day, so I don't suppose he'll be in any hurry to go to bed. He's full of it.'

She closed her eyes against the image, the ache of long-ing growing with every word. 'We'll come now,' she said. 'If that's OK? It was the first day of the new term today, and Libby goes to bed at eight on school nights. I try and stick to it if I can,' she added, trying not to sound so pathetically eager and ending up sounding like a school matron instead. Oh, grief, he was going to think she was obsessive about bedtimes...

'Now's fine. I'll give you directions.'

She scrabbled around for a piece of paper on the table and found an old envelope. 'Fire away,' she said, jotting down the address—surprisingly in the country, not in the town as she'd first thought. 'I didn't realise you lived out of town,' she said, studying the directions and trying to place the road in her mind. 'Will it take long to get there?'

'No. It's easy to find, and it's not far out. Ten minutes from the hospital, tops. I'll see you soon—and, Molly?'

'Yes?'

'He doesn't know—about you carrying him for us. I haven't told him. I'm still trying to work out how, but in the meantime I'd be grateful if you and Libby could be careful what you say.'

'Sure. Don't worry, we won't say anything. I'll see you soon.'

She cradled the phone, then sat for a moment gathering her ragged emotions. The scraping had finished, a sweet, pure sound now pouring through the door—well, mostly, she thought with a motherly smile as another tiny screech set her teeth on edge. Still, Libby wasn't quite ten yet. There was plenty of time.

The door opened and Libby bounced in, the image of her father, blonde hair bobbing round her shoulders, her pale blue eyes sparkling with achievement.

'Did you hear me?' she said. 'I did it!'

'I heard,' Molly said, her heart swelling with pride. 'Well done, your father would have been proud of you. And talking of fathers, I meant to tell you, I saw Jack's father today. He's working at the hospital.'

Libby's head tipped on one side. 'Jack's father? Your baby Jack?'

She nodded. 'Well, not mine, but yes.'

The girl's eyes sparkled even brighter. 'Cool! Can we see him? I only saw him that once when he was born, and it was ages ago.'

'Three years—and, yes, we can see him. Tonight—in fact now. If you're OK with it?'

'Sure. Can we go?'

Molly laughed and stood up. 'Yes. Brush your hair, it's a mess, and make sure you've put your violin away properly.'

'Yes, Mother,' she teased, but she bounced out and reappeared a moment later, her hair sort of brushed and the violin case in hand. 'I'm ready.'

Molly picked up the directions, read them through again and put them in her pocket. 'OK. But, remember, he doesn't know anything about me being his tummy-mummy, so don't say anything.'

Libby's eyes widened. 'He doesn't know? How weird. Laura knows, she talks about it all the time.'

Molly thought of her other surrogate child, with whom she had an affectionate and loving relationship, and smiled gently. 'Yes, I know—but Jack doesn't, and it isn't really our place to tell him.'

'It's OK, I won't say anything,' Libby promised.

'There's another thing you ought to know—his mum died.'

Libby's face fell. 'Oh, poor baby,' she said, her soft heart so typically responding to his loss. 'Still, he can have you now,' she suggested, her face brightening again.

If only, Molly thought, the ache returning. Libby would love to put the world to rights, but unfortunately it just wasn't that easy.

The drive, however, was easy, his house simple to find and really not at all far from the hospital, as he'd promised. It was a lovely house, a simple, red-brick cottage-style farmhouse, with a porch in the middle and windows all around. A rambling rose, intertwined with a late-flowering honeysuckle, scrambled over the porch, and tacked on one end of the house under a lower section of roof was what looked like another little cottage, with its own white front door, and she guessed this was where Debbie and Mark lived.

Bathed in the sunshine of a late summer evening, it looked homely and welcoming, and just the sort of place she could imagine him living in. Nothing like their London house, but she'd never felt that had been him.

The garden was bursting with colour and scent, a real cottage garden, and as they walked up the path she bent to smell the last of the roses, just as Sam opened the door.

She straightened and laughed. 'Sorry. I can't resist roses.'

'Nor can I. They're why I bought the house.' His gaze dropped and he gave her daughter a friendly smile. 'Hello, Libby, nice to see you again. How are you?'

'OK. I like your garden, it smells lovely.'

'It does, doesn't it? I can't take any credit for it. It was like this when we moved, and Debbie does all the gardening anyway. Come in, Jack's in the kitchen, "washing up" with her.' He held up his hands and drew speech marks in the air with his fingers as he spoke, and his face said it all.

'Oh, dear,' Molly said, biting her lip at the laughter in his eyes, and they exchanged a smile that made her knees go weak. Oh, lord, this was such a bad idea. She was going to get herself in such a mess.

She followed him down the hall, Libby at his side, and as he ushered her into the kitchen she came to an abrupt halt, her hand coming up to cover her mouth, her eyes filling.

No. She wasn't going to cry, she wasn't.

'Jack, come and say hello to some friends of mine,' Sam was saying, but she couldn't move, she just stood there and devoured the little boy with her eyes as he climbed down off the chair and ran over to them.

He was so tall! So tall and straight, and the image of his father, with those same astonishing blue eyes filled with laughter, and a mop of soft, dark hair that fell over his forehead, just like Sam's.

He tipped his head back and looked up at her, examining her unselfconsciously. 'Hello. I'm Jack,' he said unnecessarily, and she crouched down to his level and dredged up an unsteady smile.

'Hi. I'm Molly, and this is Libby, my daughter.' She looked at his sodden front and resisted the urge to gather him to her chest and squeeze him tightly. 'I hear you're helping with the washing-up.'

He nodded, his little head flying up and down, grinning from ear to ear. 'I do spoons, and we make bubbles.'

'We've got a dishwasher, but it's not as much fun, and this way the floor gets washed, too,' Sam said, laughter in his voice.

She chuckled at the words and straightened up, her gaze finally going past Sam and meeting the clear, assessing eyes of a woman in her late twenties. Her hair was spiky and an improbable shade of pink, and she was dressed in faded old jeans and an orange T-shirt that clashed violently with her hair. She looked like a tiny and brightly coloured elf, but, despite being so small, she radiated energy.

'You must be Debbie,' Molly said.

The woman nodded, and tipped her head towards the window. 'This is my husband, Mark.'

She turned her head and saw him for the first time, sitting quietly in a chair in front of the long, low window, one leg propped up on a stool and a cat curled up on a riotous heap of wool in his lap. The sun glinted on an armoury of piercings, and there was an elaborate tattoo running up one arm and disappearing under his sleeve.

The unlikely tapestry designer, of course.

She smiled across at him. 'Hi, there. Nice to meet you. Sam's told me a lot about you both.'

'Oh, dear, sounds ominous,' Debbie said, laughing and scooping Jack up to sit him on the table and strip off his soggy T-shirt. 'I think you'd better put something dry on, don't you? You'll catch a cold—and don't tell me it's an old wives' tale,' she said, levelling a finger at Sam.

He threw up his hands in mock surrender and pulled out a chair. 'Molly, have a seat,' he said, and she sat, quickly, before her suddenly rubbery legs gave way.

'Thanks,' she said, shooting him a grateful glance, and he smiled down at her understandingly.

'Any time. Can I get you a drink?'

'Only tea or coffee, as I'm driving,' she said, her eyes fixed on Jack's small body, taking in the strong, straight limbs, the sticky-out ribs so typical of little boys who didn't sit still long enough to gather any fat. The need to hug him close was an overwhelming ache, and she had to fold her arms and lock them to her sides to stop herself.

'I'll make coffee,' Sam was saying. 'Mark? Debbie?'

'Not for me. I'll have one when I've finished in here,' Debbie said, tugging a clean T-shirt over Jack's head, and Mark shook his head, too.

'Another ten minutes and I get my pint,' he said with a grin. 'I think I'll hold on for that.'

So Sam made coffee for Molly and himself, and poured juice for the children, and then, because it was such a lovely evening, they went out into the garden and sat amongst the scent of the roses and honeysuckle and listened to the droning of the bees while the children played in the sandpit a few feet away.

'What a gorgeous spot,' Molly said, delighted to know that Jack was living in such a lovely place. She and Libby lived in a very pleasant house with a pretty garden, in a tree-lined street convenient for the hospital and Libby's school, but it was nothing like this. Sam's house was only ten minutes from the hospital, fifteen from the town centre, and yet the peace and quiet were astonishing. They could have been miles from anywhere, she thought with a trace of envy, and then quickly dismissed it.

It wouldn't have been nearly so convenient for them, particularly not for Libby, and Molly didn't want to spend her life driving her daughter backwards and forwards every time she wanted to see a friend or visit her grandparents. It was hard enough fitting in Libby's schedule around her own work timetable without having to factor in being a taxi service.

No, living in the town suited them, but she was still glad for Jack that he would grow up with the song of the birds drowning out the faint hum of the bypass in the distance.

'So, what do you think of him?' Sam asked softly, and she dragged her eyes from the little boy who wasn't her son and smiled unsteadily across at him.

'He's gorgeous. Bright and lovely and...'

She broke off, unable to continue, and she looked away quickly before she disgraced herself.

'It's OK, Molly. I feel the same about him, so I do understand you.'

'Do you?' she said quietly. 'I'm not sure I do. He's not my son. Why do I feel like this for him?'

'Because you gave him life?'

'No. You and Crystal gave him life. I just incubated him until he was big enough to cope alone.'

'Don't underestimate your part in it. Without you he wouldn't be here. I think that gives you the right to feel emotional the first time you see him in three years.'

She closed her eyes against the welling tears. 'I've thought about him so much,' she confessed softly.

'You should have seen him,' Sam said, his voice gruff. 'I should have kept in touch, no matter what Crystal said. I wasn't happy with it. I always felt she was wrong, and I should have done something about it. I'm sorry.'

Molly shook her head slowly. 'She was his mother. She had the right to make that choice,' she pointed out, determined to defend the dead woman's decision even though it had torn her apart, but Sam made a low sound of disgust in his throat.

'She didn't want to be his mother,' he said, his voice tight and dangerously quiet. 'She went back to work when he was four months old, because she was bored at home. Seven months later she went off with her boss on a business trip to the Mediterranean, and she never came back. Her son wasn't even a year old, and already she'd turned her back on him.

'She wanted a life in the fast lane, and that was how she died—with her lover, on a jet-ski, late one night. They smacked into the side of a floating gin palace that was just coming into the harbour at Antibes and they were killed instantly. They'd both been drinking.'

Molly stared at him, shocked at the raw emotion in his voice, the anger and pain that had come through loud and clear even though his voice had been little more than a murmur. Without thinking, she reached out to him, laying her hand on his arm in an unconscious gesture of comfort.

'Oh, Sam, I'm so sorry.'

He looked down at her hand, then covered it with his and gave her a sad, crooked smile before releasing her hand and pulling his arm away, retreating from her sympathy. 'So was I. It was a hell of a way to find out my wife was being unfaithful to me.'

'Didn't you know?'

He shifted slightly, moving away as if even that small distance made him less vulnerable. 'That they were lovers? I suppose I should have done. The signs were clear enough, although she'd never told me in as many words, but, no, I didn't know. She'd been itching to get back to work from the moment Jack was born, apparently, but she'd never really said so. Like everything else, she just let me find out.'

'But—why?' Molly asked, stunned that anyone could keep secrets in a marriage. It wouldn't have occurred to her to keep anything from Mick.

'Just her way.' He pursed his lips thoughtfully. 'I suppose the first hint I had that things weren't all sweetness and light was when I came home one day and found an au pair installed—so we'd have a resident babysitter, she told me. She wanted to go out at night to glitzy restaurants where you pay a small ransom for a miserable little morsel of something unpronounceable, when I was coming home exhausted from work and just wanted to fall asleep in front of the television with my son in my arms.'

'So who won?'

He gave a sad, bitter little laugh. 'Who do you think? Crystal wanted to go out—and what Crystal wanted, Crystal got. She said she had cabin fever—said she could understand how women got postnatal depression.'

'And did it make any difference?'

Again the low, bitter laugh. 'No, of course not. Then a few days later I opened a letter addressed to her by mistake. It was a credit-card bill, and in three weeks she'd run up thousands—and I mean thousands, literally. I went upstairs and looked in her wardrobe, and tucked in amongst the clothes she already had were loads of new things I'd never seen—sexy little dresses, trouser suits, skirts, tops, all designer labels, all from the big Knightsbridge stores—the sort of thing you'd wear if you wanted to seduce your boss.'

'And it worked, I take it.'

'Oh, yes. I confronted her about the clothes, and she cried and said she was miserable at home, and of course she loved Jack, but she just wanted to get back to work, she missed it. They were work clothes, she said. She had to look the part. So I paid the credit-card bill, and she went back to work, and the rest, as they say, is history.'

She wanted to reach out again, to comfort him again, but he'd withdrawn from her and she couldn't. Instead she concentrated on watching the children, wondering how much this fractured upbringing had affected Jack.

Would she have had him for them if she'd known what had been in store? She'd had doubts about Crystal, but only when it had been too late, towards the end of her pregnancy. Had it been a mistake to hand him over at birth?

And then she heard Jack laugh, and saw the happy smile on his face and the love on Sam's as he watched his son play, and she knew it hadn't been a mistake, any of it.

Mick had died, too, although their stories couldn't have been more different, but the result was the same and Libby was now in the same boat as Jack. Molly could never have said that having her daughter had been a mistake, or regretted her birth for a moment.

No, she had done the right thing for Jack. It was Crystal who had failed him, not her, and Sam was certainly making a good job of parenting him now, as she'd known he would.

She looked at her watch. 'It's getting late,' she murmured, and Sam nodded.

'Yes. I suppose they both ought to go to bed soon. Have another coffee before you go—just a quick one.'

And so she did, just because he didn't seem to want her to leave and Libby and Jack were getting on so well, and in any case, given a choice she would have sat there all night watching Jack and absorbing every little detail about him.

She followed Sam back into the kitchen, deserted now that Debbie and Mark had gone to their own rooms in the little cottage on the end of the house, and as Sam made the coffee, she watched the children through the window.

'Penny for them.'

She shook her head. 'Nothing, really. It's just so good to see him. I just want to hug him…'

Molly broke off and turned away, but before she could move far she was turned gently but firmly back and wrapped in a pair of strong, hard arms that gathered her against his chest and cradled her in his warmth.

The sob that had been threatening since she'd arrived broke free, and he shushed her gently and rocked her against his body, and gradually she felt her emotions calming, soothed by the comfort of his arms.

'OK now?' he asked, his voice gruff, and easing back from her he looked down into her eyes.

She nodded, dredging up a watery smile, and Sam lifted his hands and carefully smudged away the tears with his thumbs.

'That's better,' he said, a smile hovering round his eyes, but then something shifted in their clear blue depths, and she felt her heart thump against her ribs. His brows drew together in a little frown of puzzlement and he eased away, releasing her abruptly and stepping back, busying himself with the coffee.

'Um—about the photos. I'm not sure where they are.

I'll ask Debbie to dig them out. They know who you are, by the way, so you don't have to worry about what you say in front of them if Jack's not there.'

She nodded, willing her heart to slow down and her common sense to return.

If she hadn't known better, she could have sworn he'd been about to kiss her and had then thought better of it.

No, not better. She couldn't think of anything better than being kissed by him, but he obviously didn't agree, to her regret.

Still, he was probably right. Their relationship was complicated enough without throwing that particular spanner in the works, however much she might want him to, and of course he had no idea how she felt about him—how she'd felt about him for years.

They went back out to the garden and drank their coffee and talked about the hospital—nice and safe and neutral, but there was a tension between them that could have been cut with a knife, and it was almost a relief when Sam put his mug down and stood up. 'Right, time that young man went to bed, I think,' he said briskly. 'It's nearly eight.'

Molly almost leapt to her feet, quick to follow his lead. 'Good grief. I didn't realise it was so late,' she lied, and hustled Libby off the swing and towards the car.

Sam scooped Jack up, and just as she was about to get into the car, he leant over in Sam's arms and held out his arms to her.

'Kiss!' he demanded.

Swallowing the lump in her throat, she hugged him gently and received his wet little kiss with a joy that brought the emotion surging back.

'Night-night, Jack,' she said unsteadily, and met Sam's eyes. Her own must be speaking volumes, she realised, but he would understand. 'Goodnight, Sam—and thank you.'

'Any time,' he said, his voice gentle, and the concern in his eyes nearly set her off again. She got hastily into the car, fumbled with her seat belt and drove away, eyes fixed on the road.

'Are you OK?' Libby said, seeing straight through her as usual, and with a little shake of her head she pulled over, folded her arms on the steering-wheel and howled.

Libby's little hand came out and squeezed her shoulder, and Molly wrapped her hand firmly over her daughter's and squeezed back.

'Poor Mummy—you've missed him, haven't you?' she said with a wisdom way beyond her years, and Molly laughed unsteadily and nodded.

'Yes. I miss Laura, too, but at least I see her. Still, I'll be able to see Jack now, so it'll be OK. It was just such a lot all at once. I'm sorry, darling. I'm all right now.'

She pulled herself together with an effort, blew her nose and wiped her eyes, and then swapped grins with her darling daughter. She was so like Mick, so sensible, so good at understanding her, hugely generous and loving.

Crazy, but even after all this time, she still missed him. He'd had the best sense of humour, the sharpest wit, the most tremendous sense of honour.

And dignity. Despite the accident that had left him in a wheelchair, and with all the resultant dependence on others for his most intimate bodily functions, Mick had never lost his dignity, and she'd been unfailingly proud of him.

She wondered what he would have made of her decision to be a surrogate mother. She'd always thought he'd have been supportive and understanding, but he would have worried about her. She could never have done it if he'd still been alive, but he wasn't, and it had been something to do to fill the huge void that his sudden and unexpected death had left behind.

In those black months after the pneumonia had claimed him, she'd been lost. She'd cared for him for years, and suddenly there had been only her and Libby, and she'd felt useless.

She'd needed to be needed, and because of a chance remark, she'd been given an opportunity to do something to help others who were unable to have children naturally. Because of Mick's paraplegia they'd only been able to have Libby with the help of IVF, and it was only one step further to imagine the anguish of a fertile mother who, due to a physical anomaly, was unable to carry her own child.

She couldn't have done it except as a host, but neither of the two children she'd carried had been genetically hers. They'd both been implanted embryos, so handing them over hadn't been like handing over her own child. That would have been too big a wrench.

Handing Jack over and knowing she wouldn't see him again had been bad enough. It had taken her years to get over the pain, and she realised now that she had never truly recovered. If he'd been her own child, it would have destroyed her. It had nearly destroyed her anyway, but now, by some miraculous stroke of fate, he was back in her life, and she didn't intend to let him out of it ever again.

The fact that Sam would also, by definition, be part of her life as well was something she would have to deal with—and so would he.

CHAPTER THREE

'YOU'RE needed in A and E, Mr Gregory.'

He frowned. He was covering one of the other firms because the consultant was on holiday and the registrar was off sick, and, frankly, being on take again for the second day running was the last thing Sam and his registrar Robert needed. He hadn't got round to any of that paperwork yesterday afternoon, and he'd hoped to get some done this morning before his afternoon clinic. There were urgent letters...

'Can't Robert do it?' he asked, but the ward clerk shook her head.

'Sorry, he's already in Theatre, and it sounded quite urgent. The girl you saw yesterday—the one in the car who was unconscious and discharged herself?'

He was already on his way to the lift by the time she finished speaking. That girl had been a crisis brewing, and he'd been mulling her case over in his mind all night—in between remembering the look on Molly's face when she'd seen Jack, and when the little tyke had kissed her goodbye. It had haunted him all night, racked him with guilt. He should have contacted her when Crystal died—should have insisted, even earlier, that they kept in touch.

Don't go there, he told himself firmly, striding down the corridor to A and E. He palmed open the door and went through to the work station, where he was directed to Resus.

'So what's the story today?' he asked, going in.

'The same, except this time she was picked up in the

street,' Matt Jordan said tersely. 'Drugs, possibly, or some bizarre form of epilepsy, but we're getting some pretty confusing results. Positive pregnancy test, though, and we picked up a heartbeat for the baby, but it was pretty erratic. We're getting a portable ultrasound down here now, and the neurologist is on his way.'

'Still no ID?'

Matt shook his head. 'No, nothing, but the car she was found in yesterday was stolen, and she hasn't washed or changed her clothes since then, so I would guess she lives in a squat. That makes the drugs more likely, but I'm almost certain there's something else as well.'

Sam nodded. That made sense. If only he could know what was making her black out, he could make a better assessment of the baby's needs. Just then the portable ultrasound machine arrived, and within moments the baby's existence was confirmed.

'Well, she's pregnant with a single foetus, and there's a heartbeat, although it's rather weak,' the sonographer said to them. 'I can't tell you any more without the big machine.'

Just then the alarm on the heart monitor went off, and Matt swore softly under his breath.

'Damn, she's arrested.'

The team moved smoothly in to start CPR, but Sam was unhappy. After two minutes of frenzied activity, she was still showing no signs of recovery, and the baby was bound to be suffering from lack of oxygen by now, even with their best attempts to support her circulation.

'How's it looking?' he asked tersely.

'Lousy. I can't worry about the baby, I'm going to have to shock her,' Matt said. 'There's still a chance we can get her back, and if this is drugs, the baby's chances are pretty slight anyway.'

Sam nodded agreement and stood back, watching grimly as they fought—and failed—to save her.

He checked the clock on the wall and sighed. They'd been working on her for nearly half an hour, and there was no way the baby was still viable, he didn't think.

He took the business end of the portable ultrasound and ran it over her abdomen, but the heartbeat they'd detected before was gone, just a shadow remaining to show the position of the heart. The baby itself was motionless.

'Damn,' he said under his breath, then straightened up. 'OK, forget the baby. We've lost it.'

And not only the baby. Despite the continuous external cardiac massage, shocking her, ventilating her, injecting her heart with adrenaline, still they were unable to get her back.

With a muttered oath Matt Jordan stripped off his gloves and looked up at the clock. 'OK, everybody. That's enough. Agreed?'

They nodded. 'Time of death ten thirty-eight,' he said, and scrubbed a tired hand through his hair. 'If only she'd stayed in yesterday, given us a chance to assess her.'

'She didn't. You can't hold people against their will,' Sam pointed out. 'There are too many damned if onlys in this job.'

He stripped off his gloves and gown, and after attending to the necessary paperwork he headed back towards Maternity, sick with the tragic waste of two young lives. Maybe the post-mortem would reveal why she'd died, but in the meantime he needed to get back to the paperwork on his other patients, finish those letters off.

Then maybe he'd have time for coffee with Molly, if she was free.

He growled under his breath. Molly. She was all he

could think about, all he could focus on. It was going to drive him mad, if he wasn't there already.

'Mr Gregory?'

He paused and turned, and there behind him was a man of his own age, the badge on his white coat declaring him to be Mr Nick Baker, Accident and Emergency Consultant. He'd seen him in Resus a few minutes ago, dealing with another patient. Now he'd followed him, for whatever reason.

'Mr Baker—what can I do for you?'

'It's Nick.'

'Sam.' He shook the man's hand, his eyes making a rapid inventory while he waited for him to come to the point. Slightly shorter than Sam, his hair was rumpled as if he'd run his hands through it, and he had laughter lines bracketing extraordinary blue eyes, but there was no laughter in evidence now. His smile was taut, and didn't reach his eyes.

'It's about my wife—she's a patient of yours. She was under Will Parry, but he moved away, so you've inherited her. I don't know if you've seen her notes, but I just wanted to fill you in.'

'Sure—of course. Is there something I should know?'

He nodded. 'She—we—lost a baby eight, nearly nine years ago. She had a congenital heart defect, and she was born at thirty-two weeks. This is our first child since, and—uh—'

'You're worried.'

His smile was wry. 'Yes—just a bit. Sally's thirty-five weeks now, and she's been scanned in London because of the problems the other baby had, and everything seems fine with this baby's heart, but—well, you know what it's like once you've had a setback of any sort, and seeing that girl in there just now...'

Sam laid a reassuring hand on his shoulder and squeezed gently. 'Don't worry. I'll look up her notes, and I'll watch out for her in clinic—when's she due in again?'

'Next week—Thursday, three o'clock.'

'I'll make sure I see her—and come with her, if you can get away. In the meantime I'll make sure that they call me in if she's admitted. In fact, I'll do one better than that. I'll give you my phone numbers—home and mobile—so you can get me at any time. OK?'

Relief flooded Nick's eyes, and he nodded, his mouth tightening. 'Thanks. I hate making such a fuss, but—'

'Forget it. I think you have a right—just as I think there's no need for you to worry either, from what you've said. I'll go and look up her notes, so I'm totally familiar with them.' He patted his pockets and came up empty-handed. 'I'll have to phone you with the numbers, I don't have anything on me to write on, but don't worry, I will do it today.'

'Thanks.'

With one last reassuring smile, Sam turned and headed up to Maternity, his mind returning inevitably to Molly.

He ran up the last flight of stairs to the department just as she emerged through the double doors. She saw him and her face lit up in one of those amazing smiles, and his heart slammed against his ribs.

Dear God, she was lovely—and he wanted her in a way he hadn't wanted a woman for years.

'Hi. I'm just going for coffee,' she said. 'Got time to join me?'

He thought of his paperwork, thought of the young mother lying dead in the hospital mortuary, her poor baby gone with her. The paperwork would still be there later, and there was nothing, sadly, that any of them could do for the girl and her unborn child. He'd ring Nick Baker with his numbers when he went back to his office, but in the meantime...

'Yes, I've got time,' he said, and turning on his heel he went back down the stairs with her at his side.

'What's wrong?'

Sam looked up and she saw a lingering sadness in the depths of his eyes. 'Oh, I've just lost my first patient here—that young woman I asked you to phone about yesterday, the one who discharged herself?'

She nodded. 'What was it?'

'Don't know. Drugs? Something neurological? Whatever, she arrested, and she didn't make it.'

'And the baby?' she asked, knowing the answer, her soft heart reaching out to the poor little thing.

'No chance. Even without all the other strikes against it, the mother was a smoker and obviously had something else going on, either a habit or an illness that affected her health, so even if we'd got it out, the baby was probably doomed. It certainly wasn't very big, so it might not have been viable yet anyway. I don't know, the post-mortem will tell us the rest of the story, hopefully.'

He dragged in a deep breath and sat back, studying her thoughtfully over the top of his mug. 'So, how are you?'

'Me?' Molly laughed a little self-consciously, remembering her rather hasty departure from his house the previous evening. 'OK. Thanks for last night.'

His smile was gentle and understanding—too understanding. 'Any time,' he said, then added softly, 'You did very well. It can't have been easy.'

'Oh, it wasn't,' she confessed with a rueful smile. 'Jack's wet little kiss did me in. I didn't get far down the road before I had to pull over. Libby was wonderful.'

'She is wonderful. She's a lovely girl.'

'She's just like Mick—so many of his best qualities, and none of my failings, thank God.'

He chuckled. 'I'm sure she has failings.'

'Oh, yes—but not mine. Not sloth and disorganisation and paranoia.'

He laughed again. 'Are you paranoid?'

'Only about things that matter,' she admitted. 'Things like safety and being honest and being fair.'

'And bedtime,' he teased, and she felt herself colour.

'I'm not really paranoid about bedtime,' she told him. 'It's just if you don't have rules, you let things stretch further and further and that isn't good for anyone.'

'You're so sensible.'

She laughed a little awkwardly. He wouldn't have said that if he'd been privy to her dreams last night, but that was between her and her maker, and there was no way he was getting an inkling! She changed the subject swiftly.

'I've got something to tell you. Did you know that Liz and David—the prolapsed-cord people—are calling their son Samuel after you? It was apparently on their list, and, since you saved his life yesterday, they thought it was appropriate.'

Sam chuckled. 'It's probably more appropriate than Lucy, anyway.'

Molly laughed. 'Probably.' She glanced at her watch. 'I need to go. I've got a mum hotting up a little—I know I've got my bleeper, but it's her third, and I have an idea that when things start moving, they'll go so fast I won't even get the gloves on before the baby arrives!'

'Well, enjoy it. Nothing like a nice, uncomplicated birth and a healthy baby to set the world to rights.'

She smiled at him gently. 'Feel free to join us if you need a little therapy.'

His answering smile was crooked. 'You know, I might
.just do that,' he said.

- She left him finishing his coffee and went back up to
Maternity, arriving just in the nick of time as her patient,
Christine, suddenly shifted up a gear or three and went
into the second stage, without bothering with transition
except to retch quietly and tell her husband she was never
speaking to him again.

Ten minutes later they had their baby, a beautiful little
girl, the daughter they'd longed for, and in the midst of
the tears and laughter Molly turned and found Sam standing by the door, a wistful smile on his lips.

Their eyes met and he pulled a face and grinned.

'Feel better?' she asked softly, and he chuckled.

'Yes, thank you. You obviously don't need me. I'll see
you later.'

He went out, leaving her to attend to her patient with a
little glow of satisfaction and the warmth of his smile still
curled around her heart.

The unknown woman had died of a cocktail of drugs complicated by a massive brain tumour. She'd probably been
taking the drugs to dull the pain—either that or she'd been
on them anyway. Whatever, the combination had been
enough to kill her, and so far, two days later, they were
still no nearer knowing who she was.

A photograph of her was put on the television news, but
nobody came forward, and Sam couldn't believe that a girl
so young could die such a lonely and unmourned death.

The police were running missing persons' checks, using
DNA and fingerprints as well as the photograph to try and
identify her, and hopefully that would yield some results.

Sam felt for the little boy who would have been her son.
At least Jack had a father who loved him, and Debbie and

Mark to care for him, and now Molly was back in his life. That poor baby would have had nobody—no history, nothing to tell him where he'd come from. How would that feel as an adult?

Hideous. Lonely, isolating—unbearably sad. Still, it was all academic, because the baby wouldn't get the chance to find out. One comforting thought was that he'd been too young to be viable, so even doing an emergency section to get him out wouldn't have helped.

Sam sat on the edge of Jack's bed and looked down at the sleeping child, and felt a great welling of love rise up inside him. His son was sometimes the only thing that kept him sane, and although there were other times when Jack nearly drove him to distraction, Sam couldn't imagine life without him.

And it was all thanks to Molly.

With a quiet sigh he stood up and went downstairs, not to the sitting room—so big, so empty—but into the sanctuary of his study. After the kitchen, it was fast becoming his favourite room in the house, and he used it as a bolt-hole when things got too much.

He had a comfortable old sofa in there, and a bookcase full of well-thumbed old favourites, and a pile of his favourite easy-listening CDs next to a little sound system.

There was an Eva Cassidy album in the CD player, and he pressed the 'play' button, dropped into a corner of the sofa and closed his eyes with a grunt of relief. The day was officially over. When he could be bothered he'd get up and go and pour himself a glass of wine, but for now he was content just to sit and listen to Eva's soft, haunting voice filtering through the speakers, and do nothing.

There were lights on in the house—a dim glow from an upstairs window, lights at Debbie's and Mark's end, and a welcoming glow from the room to the left of the front door.

Molly walked slowly up the path, pausing to glance in through that inviting window. There was a cat on the window-sill, and it eyed her with supercilious disinterest for a moment before turning away. Smiling to herself, she looked past it and into the room, and the smile softened.

Sam was lying on the sofa, his feet up on one end, his head propped against the arm at the other, and she could hear music playing softly in the background. He looked utterly relaxed and completely at home, and at first she thought he was asleep, but then she noticed one big toe moving in time to the music.

She stepped closer, reaching out to tap lightly on the glass, and his eyes opened and he turned his head towards her.

'Molly.'

She didn't hear, just saw his mouth form the word, and then the smile of welcome curved his lips and softened the harsh lines bracketing his mouth.

He went out of the room, and they arrived at the front door simultaneously, both speaking at once.

'I'm sorry to come unannounced—'

'It's good to see you—'

They laughed softly, and he drew her in, taking her arm and ushering her through the door and down the hall. 'We'll go in the sitting room,' he suggested, and she glanced at the lit doorway behind him.

'Can't we go in there?' she said wistfully. 'It looked so inviting as I walked up the path.'

'It's a mess,' he warned, but she didn't care.

'It doesn't matter. I'm not here to check on your house-keeping skills.'

He laughed. 'That's a good job. They're slight in the

extreme, and the only thing Debbie's allowed to do in there is vacuum the floor.' He didn't go in there, though, but led her through to the kitchen, put the kettle on and then turned and propped himself against the front of the Aga and tipped his head on one side, eyeing her thoughtfully.

'So—bearing in mind I'm pleased to see you whatever the reason, *was* there a reason for your visit, or is it just a social call?'

'Oh.' Molly coloured slightly, feeling suddenly a little awkward. 'I was at a loose end, and I was passing. I just thought—you said something about videos.'

Sam pulled a face. 'Oh, Molly, I'm sorry. I still haven't found them. I think they might be in a box in the loft, but I still haven't got round to looking, to be honest. We can go and look now, if you like?'

She shook her head and backed towards the door, not wanting to crowd him. 'Don't worry. Any time will do. I was literally passing—I've just dropped Libby off with my parents for the weekend. I'm on a late tomorrow, and I'm working the weekend, so she's with them from tonight. I just thought, as I was so close...'

'Sorry. Still, at least you haven't had a wasted journey over here. I will try and find them, I promise. Can I get you a drink anyway? I've put the kettle on, but I can offer you juice, or wine, or whatever.'

'Coffee?'

'Sure—unless...' He shrugged. 'If you want, we could share a bottle of wine and you could stay the night, if you don't have a pressing reason to get home.'

Her heart crashed against her ribs. Stay? With him?

'I've got two spare rooms,' he went on, 'and I keep them permanently made up. Jack's in bed, Debbie and Mark are off duty and I was about to break open a bottle, but I hate drinking alone. If you aren't on until late tomorrow, we could have a dig around in the loft, settle down for a long and self-indulgent session in front of the television and watch Jack's videos from start to finish.'

Molly was so tempted.

Tempted by Sam, tempted by the company. Above all, tempted by the thought of seeing all those images of her son—no, not her son. Jack.

And Sam's intentions seemed totally honourable.

Unfortunately.

No. She mustn't think like that. Keep it simple.

'Are you sure?' she asked, in no hurry to go home to her empty house and stare in disinterest at the indifferent summer offerings on the television. She could do the ironing or weed the garden, but this—well, this was so much more appealing.

'Of course I'm sure. The evenings get a bit lonely sometimes,' he admitted, and there was a flash of something in his eyes that her soft heart recognised and reached out to.

She smiled, and one heavy brow quirked upwards in enquiry.

'So—was that a yes, then?'

She laughed. 'Yes—please, if you don't mind. I won't stay, but I can have one glass of wine, and I'd love to sit and wallow in the videos. I know there are a million things I should be doing instead, but...'

She broke off with a shrug, and he shot her a crooked grin and shrugged away from the Aga, sliding the kettle off the hob and putting the lid down. 'Tell me about it,' he said drily. 'Right—first stop the loft, then back to the kitchen for the bottle of wine, then wall-to-wall baby videos.'

*   *   *

She should have expected to feel emotional watching it, but somehow the video of Jack's birth brought back so many deeply buried feelings that she was utterly unprepared.

Crystal was wielding the camera, and there were some candid shots that she could have lived without, but it was the expression on Sam's face in the recording as he encouraged and supported her through her labour that she found most revealing.

She'd been a little preoccupied at the time and so she hadn't really noticed how he'd reacted, although she'd been hugely reliant on his presence throughout. And when Jack had been born, he'd made no attempt to hide his very evident emotion.

She hadn't realised that. She'd been too busy trying to hide her own to worry about anyone else's, and, anyway, her attention by then had all been on the baby.

And he, of course, had been handed to her initially, and then once the cord had been cut, to Crystal.

Sam had taken over filming at that point, until Jack's screams had got to them all and the midwife had taken him from his uneasy mother and handed him to Sam. He'd given Crystal back the camera, and she'd caught the moment when Sam had taken his son in his arms for the first time.

The screams had stopped, settling to soft, unhappy hiccups and then to silence, and Molly had met Sam's proud and tear-filled eyes and had slowly nodded her approval.

That, she realised, was the moment when she'd relinquished the child who wasn't her son—the child she'd nurtured and supported from the moment he'd been implanted into her womb, the child she'd felt kick and squirm inside her for all those long months until the moment of his birth.

She'd handed him over, as agreed—but not to his

mother, she acknowledged now in a moment of astonishing clarity. She'd given him to his father, instinctively realising that he was the one she could trust with this precious gift.

Was that why Jack had stopped crying? Because he, too, had instinctively trusted his father? Or was it because Sam was used to handling babies and was more confident with him?

She didn't know, and it didn't really matter now, she supposed. Not after so many other things had happened in his short life.

Molly felt something splash on her hand, then again, and she realised in surprise that she was crying. Not sobbing, just—crying, tears streaming down her cheeks as she watched the fractured images and remembered.

'Here,' Sam said gruffly, and she felt him press a tissue into her hand.

He didn't touch her—didn't hug her or offer any words of comfort, and for that she was grateful, because she would simply have fallen apart. Instead he crouched down in front of the video machine and swapped tapes while she scraped her ragged emotions together and mopped herself up.

Then he sat down again beside her, put her glass of wine in her hand and settled back.

'Do you want to stop?'

She shook her head. 'No. No, I'm fine. It was just—it brought it all back.'

He nodded slowly. 'I know. I haven't seen it before. Crystal put it away.'

His voice sounded rough, unused, and it dawned on her that he might have left her alone in order to be alone himself—that maybe crouching down in front of the television had been to give himself time to recover, as much as her.

Had the images of Crystal hurt him? Did he still love her, despite the way she'd behaved before her death?

She didn't know, and it didn't seem appropriate to ask, but her heart reached out to him. She'd been devastated when Mick had died, and nothing but time had taken away the pain.

Time, and doing what she'd done, loaning her body to bear someone else's child, so they too could experience the happiness she and Mick had shared when Libby had been born.

Except, of course, she hadn't been detached enough, even just as a host mother. She'd allowed herself to care too much about each of those babies, and although she'd stayed in touch with Laura, being denied access to Jack had torn her apart.

Or was it really Jack? Had it been Sam she'd missed, in fact, Sam she'd wanted to see so that every day had become a wasteland without his smile?

She remembered the first time she'd seen his smile, when she'd visited her friend Lynn in London after she'd given birth to her first surrogate baby. Sam had been standing beside her bed, and Lynn had looked up and said something to him, and he'd turned to her, and their eyes had met and locked.

In that moment, before she'd known what he'd want from her, before she'd had any idea of what lay ahead, some bond had been forged between them. And over the months their friendship had grown and deepened, forming a bond so deep she would have trusted him with her life. Under other circumstances, she thought—but there had been no other circumstances.

Until now.

But now was no different. Nothing had changed, he still

wasn't available. He was still in love with Crystal, she realised, and so she was destined to be hurt all over again.

'This bit's snippets of the next few weeks,' he told her, and pressed the 'play' button on the remote control. The images flickered to life on the screen, Jack in the bath, Jack having a bottle, Jack with Crystal's parents—and as the video played, Sam watched Molly out of the corner of his eye.

She seemed all right now, more composed, laughing at the funny bits when Jack was older and his character started to show.

There was a chronological jump from when he was a little under a year to almost eighteen months, the time just after Crystal had died. She'd done most of the filming up till then, something that had hardly dawned on him, and it had all been staged.

Once things had settled down after her death and he'd started filming again, it had been more spontaneous. He would grab the camera if something funny happened when he was around, and the result was predictably less tidy but warmer, somehow. Strangely, their life felt like that now— less tidy, but warmer, more spontaneous, more genuine.

What a sad indictment of Crystal's contribution to their family life.

The tape came to an end, and for a moment Molly said nothing, then she turned to him with that understanding look in her eyes that seemed to see straight through him, and said, 'You really love him, don't you?'

Sam's smile felt a little off-kilter. 'It would be hard not to,' he said, remembering even so that Crystal had seemed to manage. The thought brought a familiar pang of sadness, but he ignored it, looking instead at Molly's glass and raising an eyebrow.

'Are you sure I can't talk you into having another one and staying? You're very welcome.'

'Are you trying to get me drunk?' she asked laughingly, and then their eyes met, and need, hot and urgent and totally unexpected, ripped through him.

He dragged his eyes away. 'As if I would,' he said lightly—or tried, but his voice sounded raw and unused, and he stood up and walked over to the television, gathering together the videos and his thoughts before he disgraced himself.

'I really ought to go,' she said softly. 'Thank you so much for showing me all of them.'

'There are more—here, borrow them and watch them in your own time, there's no hurry to have them back,' he said, rising and turning towards her with two more tapes in his hand. He thrust them at her, and she took them, her eyes scanning him warily. He didn't need her looking at him that closely. God only knows what she'd see.

He went past her and opened the door, and she gathered up her things and followed him, pausing in the confines of the entrance hall to look up at him one last time.

'Thanks again,' she murmured, and before he could move, she came up on tiptoe and brushed a feather-soft kiss against his cheek.

Then she was gone, leaving nothing behind but a lingering trace of her scent and a raging desire that would taunt him for the rest of the night.

CHAPTER FOUR

MOLLY was glad she hadn't stayed the night.

Even though she found the house empty and lonely without Libby, she needed to be alone to wallow in a totally self-indulgent howl. She watched the other videos, alternately laughing and crying, and as she watched she built up an image of Jack's life.

He seemed to integrate well with other children. Birthday parties and events at his nursery in London showed him happy and well adjusted, and she realised it was largely due to Sam and his enormous warmth.

Debbie and Mark had also taken turns filming over the last year, and so there were lots of scenes with Sam himself—scenes in which Molly found herself taking a very close interest for an entirely different reason.

'You're an idiot,' she told herself, after watching one scene three times on the trot. Stabbing the 'rewind' button, she went into the kitchen and made herself a hot drink, then turned off the television and video player and went to bed.

That didn't help. She could still see him laughing helplessly at something Jack had done, and closer to home, she could feel the rough scrape of stubble against her lips as she'd kissed him goodbye.

It would have been so easy to linger, to go back for more, to kiss him on those mobile, sculpted lips that her own were crying out to touch...

With a groan of frustration she set down her cup, flicked off the light and resolutely lay down on her side, one hand under her cheek, and forced herself to relax. She knew how to do it—she spent all day showing women in labour how to let go of tension to ease their contractions.

It just wasn't working for her tonight, that was all.

Relax your jaw, she told herself, and as her teeth lost contact with each other, she felt the tension drain away. Not for long, though. Not long enough to fall asleep and escape the memory of those laughing eyes and the rasp of stubble against her cheek...

It was one of those labours.

Typical, Molly thought. It's just because I've had practically no sleep and all I want to do is crawl into a corner and hide.

'Come on, let's go for another walk around and see if we can't move things on,' she suggested to the weary mother, and helped her off the edge of the bed. They walked slowly out of the delivery room and down the ward, round the nursing station and back to the delivery room, pausing on the threshold while Kate had another contraction.

'Oh, Molly, I can't do this,' the exhausted woman said when it had passed, and Molly was beginning to wonder if she wasn't right.

The baby's presentation had been fine initially, but it was a few days overdue and from her examination Molly had felt that it was a large baby. Not that it was always possible to tell, but she had a good feel for these things and her instincts were suddenly screaming that something had changed.

It wasn't Kate's first baby. If it had been, Molly would have called Sam in before now, just to be sure there wasn't a problem with her pelvis that had been missed.

Her last baby had been born normally, without any undue fuss by all accounts, and this was her third. It should have been easy, and it wasn't. It wasn't made any easier, either, by the fact that Kate's naval husband was on a tour of duty abroad and she was having to do this alone.

'Come on, let's have another look at you,' she said. 'I've got a feeling your baby's managed to get itself jammed in your pelvis, but I can't tell without a look.'

Molly helped her back onto the bed, and the briefest examination confirmed her fears. The baby's head was crowning, ready for delivery, but it was a posterior lie, with the baby facing the front, not the back, and the baby's shoulder was jammed over the top of the pubic bone, so the poor little thing was wedged and unable to descend any further.

'OK,' she said, stripping off her gloves. 'Your baby's got itself stuck. We just need to increase the diameter of your pelvis, and to do that I need you to rock on all fours, or go up and down steps, squat sharply, rock with one foot on a stool—anything like that which will stretch out that pelvis and give it a bit more room for that shoulder to come down.'

'Will it be enough?' Kate asked doubtfully. 'I thought they broke things when that happened, or is that just a myth?'

Rats. Molly paused, then went for the truth. Kate was an educated woman and there was no point in insulting her intelligence. 'No, it isn't a myth. It might mean that the baby's collar-bone has to bend to free it, so it could end up with a little greenstick fracture, but it won't be a problem for it, and we'll immobilise it if it happens so it won't feel pain afterwards, and they heal very quickly.'

Kate closed her eyes and swallowed. 'Oh, damn,' she said unsteadily. 'How dare Pete be away when I need him?'

Molly sat on the edge of the bed and gave Kate a re-assuring hug. 'Come on, we can do this. The sooner your baby's born, the better, really, and once that shoulder slips past the pelvis, it'll be out in no time, I promise, and there's a good chance it'll be absolutely fine.'

'Right.' Kate pulled herself together and gave Molly a brave smile. 'What do you want me to do?'

Molly helped her struggle awkwardly off the bed. 'Here—we've got some big hard foam blocks we can use.'

That was how Sam found them a few minutes later, with one of Kate's feet on the edge of a block, rocking back and forth.

He arched a brow in enquiry, and Molly sent him a silent plea for help.

'Kate's baby's shoulder's managed to get stuck, and it's a posterior lie,' she said calmly. 'We're just trying to free it, but we haven't had any luck yet.'

'Have you tried a squat?'

She shook her head. 'Not yet. We were just about to.'

'Try it—here, Kate, hang on the end of the bed and squat down quickly. Molly'll steady you, and I just want to see if I can give the baby's shoulder a little help with my hand to drop it off that bone,' he suggested, and Kate obediently changed position and tried again, with Sam crouching almost under her.

He placed the heel of his hand on the baby's shoulder, just above Kate's pelvic arch, and as she squatted he pushed firmly backwards.

'Oh,' she said, and looked up, alarmed. 'I can feel something—oh, my God. It's moving— Ow!'

She sagged towards the floor, but Sam was there first, catching her before she hit the deck.

'OK, Kate, I've got you. Molly, check her while I support her here.'

'She's there, it's free. And you shouldn't be holding her like that, the health and safety executive will have your guts for garters,' she muttered under her breath, but he just grinned.

'They have to catch me first. It's OK, Kate, we'll soon have you sorted.'

He took the big inflatable gym ball Molly shoved in his direction and helped Kate drape herself over it, then knelt down behind her as Molly quickly covered the floor mats with clean sheets in the nick of time.

'Kate, pant for me, don't push,' Molly instructed, but Kate wasn't having any of it. With a feral growl, she strained down and delivered her baby without further ado.

Sam didn't have gloves on, neither did Molly. There simply wasn't time, but neither of them cared. Kate and the baby came first, and just then their concern was for the little boy who was born screaming furiously and flailing one arm and both legs.

'Clavicle,' Sam said, lifting the tiny arm and holding it in place on his chest to relieve the stress on the fractured collar-bone.

'It's a boy, Kate, and he's fine,' Molly told her, hugging her gently. 'He's lovely. Let's just sit you down and you can hold him.'

She helped Kate roll over and lean against a backrest, then Sam pulled up her gown and laid the baby against her abdomen, skin to skin.

'I'm afraid his collar-bone's cracked, but he's going to be fine,' Sam told her. 'Just hold him like that for a moment, and we'll get the paediatrician to come and look at him and strap it so he'll be more comfortable, OK? In the meantime—well done. You did well—he's a heck of a size.'

'That's my husband,' she said, staring down at her baby

with a mixture of joy and concern in her eyes. 'He's six foot four, and every inch of it solid bone and muscle. The other two were big, but not like this. Oh, well, at least his lungs are all right!'

The baby's screams had subsided the moment he was put on Kate's now soft abdomen. Following her instincts, she shifted the baby carefully towards her breast and brushed the nipple against his cheek.

Immediately he turned, taking the nipple in his mouth and sucking vigorously, and Kate looked up with tears in her eyes.

'Well, there's nothing wrong with his jaws, either,' she said laughingly, and they all chuckled, the tension in the room dissipating as the baby's loud sucking replaced the sound of his whimpers.

'What about the placenta?' Sam asked quietly, but Molly just smiled and shook her head.

'I let nature take its course in the third stage, unless I'm worried. I don't believe in using Syntocinon unless I have to. If a mum's managed everything else herself, I reckon she can usually manage that, and there's no contraindication in her previous history.'

Sam nodded, a slow smile of approval appearing in his eyes. 'Good. Well, since you don't seem to need my muscles any more, I'll leave you to it.'

'You couldn't see if you could rustle up a cup of tea for Kate, could you?' she asked with a grin, and he rolled his eyes.

'I don't know—porter, kitchen assistant. You'll have me swabbing the floors next.'

Molly looked at the trail of amniotic fluid leading from the bed to the mats, and laughed. 'Since you mention it…!'

His snort floated on the air behind him, leaving both women chuckling.

'Do you think I'll get tea?' Kate asked, a smile lingering on her lips.

'I wouldn't be surprised,' Molly told her, and, true enough, a few minutes later he reappeared with a tray, three cups of tea and a plate of biscuits.

'Oh, top man,' Molly said with a smile of thanks, and he bowed and clicked his heels.

'We aim to please. Any progress?'

'Yes, we have one placenta, all present and correct, and everything's fine.'

'Excellent.' He passed Kate her cup once Molly had shifted her onto one side so the hot liquid wouldn't be above the baby, and settled down with one hip hitched on the edge of the delivery bed and his foot dangling, swinging idly in time to some inner beat.

He looked utterly relaxed, and yet Molly knew he was watching Kate for the slightest hint of trouble.

There was none, of course. She drank her tea, her eyes never leaving the now sleeping baby, and then, while Sam cuddled him, Molly helped Kate onto the bed, checked her and did the two little sutures that were necessary.

'Right, that's you fixed and sorted,' Molly said with satisfaction, and stripped off her gloves.

The paediatrician, Josh Lancaster, appeared at that moment and grinned at them.

'Hi, there. Got a baby for me to look at?'

'Wow, we get the boss man,' Molly joked, and Josh laughed.

'I was up in SCBU and my registrar's off sick, so I thought I'd call in on the way down. Hi, I'm Josh Lancaster, one of the consultant paediatricians,' he said to Kate, then looked at her more closely. 'Don't I know you?' he asked, and she smiled.

'Yes, possibly. My oldest, Nicky, had meningitis last year.'

'Of course. Doyle, isn't it? Kate and…Peter?'

She laughed, amazement in her voice. 'That's right. I'm surprised you remembered.'

'I never forget a parent, they're my greatest asset,' he said with a grin, and perched beside her. 'So, what happened?'

'He got stuck,' Kate said in disgust. 'Poor little scrap.'

'Little?' Sam said with a gust of laughter. 'Tell it to the fairies! Have you weighed him yet, Molly?'

'Oh, yes. He's a fraction under five kilos—that's almost eleven pounds.'

Kate's eyes widened. 'Good grief,' she said faintly. 'I thought he felt big when I was holding him, but I had no idea he was that big. He feels tiny compared to the others now, but I suppose he is huge.'

Josh chuckled. 'He must take after your husband—I seem to remember he towered head and shoulders over everyone in Paediatrics.'

He stood up and took the baby carefully from Sam. Laying him on the bed at his mother's feet where she could watch his examination, he carefully assessed the baby and nodded.

'Well, everything's fine. All his reflexes are good and he's all quite normal, except for the size and this clavicle which should heal very quickly—within days, really. I'll strap it to his chest to immobilise it—Molly, could you clean him up a bit for me first?'

She didn't attempt to bath him, not with the injury, just wiped him carefully with warm, damp swabs and patted his fragile skin dry.

Minutes later his arm was secured against his chest to stop any unnecessary movement, and Josh had shown Kate how to handle the baby so as to not put any pressure on the healing bone.

By this time Sam had been bleeped and had disappeared to another patient, and when Josh went, Kate looked up at Molly and gave her a shaky smile.

'OK?' Molly asked her gently, and without warning Kate burst into tears. 'Oh, sweetheart, he'll be all right,' she crooned comfortingly, rocking both of them against her chest. 'Don't be sad. He's OK.'

'It's just a shock,' Kate said, sniffing and easing away. 'I want to see Pete…'

And she started to cry again. Molly sat back and rubbed her hip gently and let her cry. After a few minutes Kate sniffed to a halt and gave Molly a watery smile.

'I'm sorry. I feel such an idiot.'

'Don't be daft. Your husband's thousands of miles away, you've just had a difficult and traumatic delivery, and you're only human. Here.' She plonked a handful of tissues in Kate's fingers and stood up. 'Let's move you back into the other room and get you settled. You'll be more comfortable there. Can I ring anyone for you, or get you the phone so you can contact anyone?'

Kate nodded. 'The phone would be good. I can get a message to Pete—he knew I was in labour this morning, and he'll be on tenterhooks by now.'

'I'll bet,' Molly said with a laugh. 'Come on, then, let's get you settled down and you can ring him and have a nice long chat.'

Molly was exhausted. She hadn't finished work until nine, and by the time she got home it was after half past and her lack of sleep the night before was telling on her.

She was just about to fall into a chair when the phone rang, and she sighed and picked it up. 'Hello?'

'Molly? It's Sam,' he said unnecessarily. 'Are you OK?'

She gave a short laugh. 'Knackered, but fine. Why?'

She could almost hear the shrug. 'Just wondered. Have you eaten?'

'Eaten? As in food? Not that I remember,' she said with a wry smile. 'To be honest, I don't think I can be bothered to cook.'

'That's what I thought, and Debbie doesn't cook for me on Friday nights because they go out to the pub for a meal at six, so I haven't eaten either. How do you fancy a take-away?'

Frankly, all she really fancied was crawling into bed, but then her stomach rumbled and reminded her just how hungry she was—and anyway, an excuse to spend time with Sam couldn't be bad.

'Sounds good,' she said, a little bit of her wondering how she'd find the energy. 'Shall I pick one up on the way over?'

'I'll come to yours, it was my idea,' he said promptly. 'And I've found the baby photos. I'll bring them. You need to give me your address.'

'One forty-seven Rushbrook Road,' she said. 'It's—'

'I know where it is. I looked at a house there when I was buying. Is your car on the drive?'

'Yes. The house is on the left as you head out of town, and the number's on the gate.'

'OK. Give me fifteen minutes. Chinese or Indian?'

'Don't care,' she said, placing her hand flat over her howling stomach to suppress it. 'Whatever's nearest to you—Chinese, probably. There's one on the roundabout near the hospital. Why don't you call them in advance? I can give you the number.'

'I tell you what, why don't you call them and order

whatever you fancy, and I'll pick it up? Get lots, I'm starving, and there's nothing I don't like.'

Lots, he said? Molly ordered a set meal for two with other bits and pieces, her stomach causing a ruckus through the entire procedure, and then to pass the time until he arrived she threw her breakfast things into the dishwasher, put some plates to warm and went round the sitting room like a whirling dervish, patting cushions and clearing up Libby's scattered possessions.

Not that it mattered what he thought of her house, of course, but she was suddenly and belatedly afflicted with an attack of house-pride, and of course she'd been saving the housework to do this weekend while Libby was away.

Sam arrived just as she was realising how bad the house was, and with a sigh of resignation she went to the door and opened it.

He was standing there with a white plastic carrier bag and a lazy, sexy grin. 'I take it you're hungry, too,' he said, brandishing the carrier bag, and stepped over the threshold, stooping to brush her cheek with his lips in passing.

Her heart stopped, then started again with a crash.

Food, she thought. Talk about the food.

'Well, you said lots,' she reasoned, trying to ignore the thrashing pulse in her throat and the jiggling in her stomach caused by his very presence. He'd shaved this evening, she noticed. His chin, as it had grazed her cheek, was smoother than his jaw had been the other night—gracious, last night.

Had it been only last night she'd sat up with him and watched the videos?

She led him through to the kitchen and pulled out a chair at her kitchen table—much smaller than his, and altogether less lovely, but all that would fit in her house—and waved him towards it.

'Here, sit down, the kitchen's not big enough for two people standing up,' she told him, and pulled the plates out of the oven, putting them down in front of him. He was unpacking the carrier bag, lifting out carton after carton of wonderful-smelling food, and her stomach rumbled loudly.

He laughed. 'Well, that answers that question,' he said with a grin, and pulled a bottle out of his pocket. 'Here—wine. I can only have one glass, but I'm sure you can finish it up on your own at some point.'

Molly would have drunk it all there and then in one swallow if she'd thought it would settle her gyrating heart. Instead she settled for handing him two glasses and the corkscrew while she opened the cartons and found some cutlery and the soy sauce.

For a while there was silence. Not an uncomfortable silence, but the dedicated and companionable silence of two hungry people sharing a meal together. Finally Sam laid down his fork and threw his hands in the air in defeat.

'I submit,' he said, laughing. 'I'll die if I eat any more.'

'Me, too,' she agreed, pushing away the remains of her third plateful. 'More wine?'

He shook his head. 'No, I mustn't, I'm driving. Don't let that stop you, though.'

Was it the wine, or his presence? Whatever, her guard was down. She made him coffee and poured herself another glass of wine, and they went through to the sitting room. He settled down on one end of the sofa and patted the cushion beside him, his face impassive.

'Photos,' he said, and she sat next to him and tried to maintain a distance, but it was impossible. She had to lean over to see the photos, and within a minute or two she'd ended up with her shoulder resting against his arm and her head so close to his their hair was touching.

She could feel the warmth of his body seeping into her, and she ached to snuggle up against him and absorb his warmth and companionship.

More than that, of course—much more than that, but more would be greedy, and frankly she'd settle for this…

'Molly? Are you asleep?'

She shook her head and straightened up. 'No. Just tired.'

'Here.'

Sam lifted his arm and tucked her into the hollow of his shoulder, wrapping his arm around her and snuggling her close, and then he carried on sifting through the photos and telling her about them, his voice warm and low, lulling her…

Sam looked down at the sleeping woman curled against his side and swallowed hard. She looked exhausted, but peaceful. Too peaceful to move, he thought, and, stretching out his legs, he shifted down the sofa a little and drew her closer to his chest.

Molly snuggled down, and he took the opportunity to study the room. It was very comfortably furnished, full of little homely touches that made him feel like an intruder— like the picture on the mantelpiece of her standing with a young man on a windy clifftop, laughing up at him while her hair streamed out behind her. The same man appeared in two other photos, one a wedding photo with Molly at his side, the other with Molly and a baby. In the last two photos, he was in a wheelchair.

Mick.

His arm tightened involuntarily, and she made a tiny, sleepy noise that nearly finished him and wriggled closer still. He looked down at her, soft and warm and inviting, and all the blood in his brain migrated south in aid of a more needy cause.

He closed his eyes and dropped his head back. Down, boy, he told himself. Too complicated. Too messy. Too hot to handle.

Oh, rats, he was going to get so seriously burned!

Molly woke some time later with a crick in her neck and the imprint of Sam's shirt buttons on her cheek. She knew that, because she could feel the dents in her skin when she rubbed it.

Great. She must look wonderful, with her hair all mussed and her skin flushed and creased and her eyes half-closed and bloodshot...

His arm tightened around her, drawing her back against him. 'Where are you going?' he asked, his voice low and gravelly in her ear.

'Nowhere. I was just sitting up.'

He released her, and she straightened and stretched a little, easing out the kinks. 'I'm sorry,' she said, embarrassment dawning as she woke up more and realised just how comprehensively she'd been asleep. 'I must have been more tired than I thought. Um—what's the time?'

He glanced at his watch and blinked to clear his eyes. 'Twelve-thirty.'

'Really? Oh, I'm so sorry.'

'Don't be.'

He caught her hand and she turned to look at him, her heart suddenly clamouring again.

'I need a drink,' she said hastily, pulling away from him. 'It's the Chinese. It always makes me thirsty. All that salt.'

She stood up and went quickly out to the kitchen, hoping he wouldn't follow her, but it was too much to expect. He was there at her elbow, taking her glass after she'd finished with it and filling it again, his throat working rhythmically as he drained it.

He was close to her—too close, so she could see every pore of his skin, every short, dark hair that stubbled his jaw.

He set the glass down and sighed.

'I must go. I'll leave the photos for you—you can go through them again at your leisure. They're all on disc, so I can print you copies of the lot, if you like.'

Molly swallowed. 'Thanks. I'll look at them tomorrow. And thank you for the meal and the wine, they were lovely.'

'Put the leftovers in the fridge. You'll have enough for tomorrow—today, even.'

'And the next day—if I can ever eat again,' she said with a hollow laugh. 'I still feel full.'

'You'll live.'

Sam paused just inside the front door and turned towards her. 'Thank you for your company this evening. It was fun. Eating alone is just refuelling, really, and—well, it was nice to have someone to share it with, make it more of an occasion for a change.'

He bent to kiss her cheek, just as she moved her head to shake the hair back from her face, and their lips collided. For a second they froze, then with a ragged sigh Sam drew her into his arms, tunnelled the fingers of one hand through her hair and anchored her head as his mouth came down on hers.

She'd never really understood the word hungry before, she thought dimly. Or urgent.

Sam was both, and his hunger fuelled hers. A cry rose in her throat, trapped by his lips, and she lifted her arms and threaded her fingers through the dark, silky strands of his hair, pulling him down again when he would have retreated.

With a groan he shifted, pressing her body against the wall, his thigh hard and insistent between hers, rocking against her until she whimpered with need.

Then he lifted his head and stared down at her, swallowing convulsively and stepping back, ramming shaking fingers through his hair and leaving it rumpled and even more tempting.

'Hell, Molly, I'm sorry—I don't know what I was thinking about. Dear God, I'm so sorry...'

She pressed her fingers against his lips and shook her head. 'Don't. Don't apologise. It was as much me as you.'

He gave a snort of disbelief and shook his head to clear it. 'Molly, I—I don't know what to say.'

She smiled somehow. 'Goodnight might be sensible,' she offered pragmatically, and he laughed and drew her back into his arms, hugging her gently before releasing her and stepping back.

'You're right, of course. Goodnight, Molly. I'll see you on Monday.'

And with that he was gone, leaving her in a welter of heated emotions and cold fried rice.

She laughed, because otherwise she would have cried, and because she couldn't bear to come down and sort it out in the morning, she cleared up the kitchen, loaded the dishwasher and went up to bed.

It was going to be another restless night, she thought, but she was wrong.

Even her overindulgence couldn't disturb the peaceful slumber she fell into, and she slept dreamlessly until nine the following morning, waking refreshed, if thirsty, and ready for the day.

She attacked the house and laundry until the place was

sparkling, and then settled down with a cup of tea and a Danish pastry, courtesy of the bakery round the corner, and looked through the photos again. She just had time to flick through them before she had to go to work at three.

The ones of Jack were lovely, of course, but it was the ones of Sam that drew her again and again. One in particular, of him with his son, made her heart swell just looking at it. And in another he was grinning cheekily, and the camera had caught a sexy dimple in his cheek that made her long for things she couldn't have.

Or could she? What was there to prevent her having a relationship with Sam?

Nothing. Mick was dead, and so was Crystal. They were both free, both apparently willing, and, heaven knows, it would be wonderful to be with him and Jack. Libby would love having a father, especially one as caring and warm as Sam, and Jack needed a mother.

If not his own, then who better than the woman who'd carried him?

No. That was going too far into the future, aiming for the moon and the stars, but down here, realistically within reach, surely there was something for them? There hadn't been before, and indeed it had never even been suggested, but now—who knows? She'd loved him before, with nothing between them and no hope of anything in the future that she'd been aware of. Now, with no reason why not, she realised her love had grown.

Molly stared sightlessly at the photo of Sam. She might not be the woman he'd put top of his list, but Crystal was gone, and there was something there between them, she knew that. Did they have a chance at happiness? And if so, didn't they owe it to themselves—and the children— to take it?

She focused on the picture, taking in again the planes

and angles of his face, the crease in his cheek, the deep laughter lines around his eyes and mouth, and she thought of his face after he'd kissed her, taut with desire.

The heat in his eyes had nearly brought her to her knees, and it gave her hope. If he wanted her that much—and it seemed certain that he did—perhaps that was the way to start.

An affair—nothing more, nothing complicated, just good old-fashioned chemistry given free rein.

She laughed softly. Oh, yes. That would be good—and it was about darned time.

All she had to do now was persuade Sam…

CHAPTER FIVE

SAM could have kicked himself all the way home. Why had he kissed her?

Idiot, he growled to himself. Stupid, stupid idiot. They had to be friends, for Jack's sake, and he had no business screwing around with Molly's emotions and messing her up. She'd had enough trauma in her personal life to date without him contributing to it in a fit of adolescent hormones!

He pulled up on his drive and dropped his head back against the headrest with a heavy sigh. Lord, she'd felt so good in his arms. Soft and ripe—and willing. Oh, yes, she'd been willing—but that wasn't the point.

The fact that they were attracted to each other was irrelevant under the circumstances. Jack was the only one who mattered here, and he'd do well to remember that.

Even if it meant he never got to lose himself in her arms, to bury himself in her body and find that glorious oblivion he knew was waiting for him there...

Damn!

He slammed his hand on the steering-wheel and winced, shaking it ruefully and rubbing it to ease the inevitable bruise. He wanted her. He'd wanted her for years, ever since he'd first set eyes on her, if he was honest, although he'd never acknowledged it before, and now that they were both free it was going to be even harder to walk away.

He'd do it, though. He'd do it for Jack.

He locked the car and went inside, closing the communicating door on the landing so Debbie and Mark would know he was home. Going into Jack's room, he stared down at him for an age, just to remind himself how important his son was.

Not that he needed reminding.

Jack was lying on his back, one arm outflung, and he looked so young, so vulnerable. He was only three years old, and he'd already lost his mother. Both his mothers, in fact.

First, he'd been separated from Molly, the woman who'd borne him. Had the baby he'd been then missed her? There was no way to tell, but Sam wouldn't have been surprised. Then Crystal, his real mother, hadn't wanted to be, and had escaped her responsibilities whenever possible. Had that damaged him? Sam had done everything in his power to minimise that damage—but then, with her death, their young son had suffered the ultimate loss.

Sam couldn't expose him to any further hurt, and he wouldn't, even if it meant denying himself a relationship with Molly. He'd sooner die than hurt his child any more.

Kissing Jack lightly on the forehead, he tucked the covers round his skinny little shoulders and went to bed, only to lie there till dawn tormented by a need that went soul-deep, a need he refused to acknowledge as anything but physical.

It was just frustration. It had been over two years, after all. More than that, probably. He'd hardly touched Crystal after Jack was born because she'd withdrawn from him, and, naïve fool that he was, he hadn't realised why until it was too late.

There'd been no one since. He'd been too busy making sure that Jack's life was as smooth and happy as possible, and there'd been no time to think about what he was missing.

He was only thirty-four, though—thirty-five in November. Still young enough to burn for a woman.

And, dear God, he was burning for Molly. He closed his eyes against the morning light and rolled to his side, pulling the quilt up over his eyes. It didn't help. He could still see her, her mouth soft and swollen from his kiss, her eyes wide and vulnerable, their beautiful golden brown trusting and confused.

He swallowed hard. She'd been his for the asking. He could have been with her even now, this terrible ache burned away by the fire that would have consumed them—

'Daddy?'

He pulled the quilt down from his eyes and raised himself on one elbow, stifling a groan. 'Hello, Jack. You OK, son?'

Jack nodded, clambering up onto the bed and squirming down under the covers against his chest.

'Do you need the loo?' Sam asked him automatically, but Jack shook his head.

'Done a wee by myself. Want a cuddle,' he said, thrusting his skinny bottom towards Sam's stomach. His cold little feet settled on Sam's thighs, and the steady rise and fall of his chest slowed into sleep.

Sam's heart contracted. This was what it was all about— this was all that mattered.

Tears filled his eyes and, closing them, Sam snuggled the little body closer to his own and finally, comforted by his son's presence, he drifted off.

It was a busy week, and there weren't any chances to talk.

At least, not to say what Molly had to say to Sam, and she was beginning to wonder if there would ever be an opportunity. And gradually, as the days went by, it dawned on her that he was avoiding her.

Oh, he was perfectly polite, but instead of seeking her out for coffee, as he had done the previous week, he seemed to be permanently tied up.

So, if she wanted to talk to him, she was going to have to make it happen.

She collared him on Thursday afternoon just as he was leaving the ward, and if she'd had any doubts before, the way his eyes avoided hers laid them to rest.

'Have I done something wrong?' she asked quietly, and his eyes met hers briefly and slid away, their expression shuttered and unreadable.

'Wrong? Of course not.'

'So why are you avoiding me?'

'I'm not—'

'Don't lie to me, Sam,' she said softly. 'You owe me more than that.'

'Oh, hell.' He stabbed a hand through his hair and sighed. 'I just— Last Friday night—'

'Sam, it was just a kiss.'

He said something short and to the point, and his eyes met hers then, their expression far from shuttered this time. She felt a warm tide of colour sweep her skin, starting at her feet and working up steadily to her hairline, and it was her turn to look away.

She didn't let herself, though, not for more than a second. 'I wanted to talk to you,' she said, taking her courage in both hands. 'When can we meet? Alone?'

'I'm not sure that's a good idea.'

She sighed. 'Sam, we're both adults.'

'That's the trouble,' he admitted, and this time when their eyes met they held. After a moment he let his breath out on a gusty sigh and rammed a hand through his hair again, defeat showing in every line of his body. 'OK. Whenever. I've got the resident babysitter, you tell me.'

'Saturday afternoon? Libby's got a birthday party from two in the afternoon. I don't have to pick her up until ten on Sunday morning.'

Something—heat or panic—flared in his eyes, and he looked away. 'OK. I'll come to you—say, three o'clock?'

She nodded. 'Fine. I'll make a cake.'

He made a strangled sound that could have been disbelieving laughter, and backed away, heading for the door. 'I have to go—I'm meeting a patient and her husband, and they're waiting for me. I'll see you later.'

'I'm off duty now until Monday. I'll see you on Saturday.'

He nodded, turned and strode away from her, and Molly got the unsettling feeling that if he could have outrun his thoughts, he would have done exactly that.

They make a good-looking couple, Sam thought as he walked down through the antenatal clinic to his office. He wondered why they'd waited eight years before trying for another child, but there was nothing in the notes to indicate they'd had trouble conceiving.

Was it just anxiety that had made them hold back?

They saw him coming and got to their feet, and he held out his hand in greeting, a smile coming readily to his lips. 'Sally, it's good to meet you. Glad you could make it, Nick. Come on into my office.'

He ushered them in, closed the door and waved at the chairs in front of his desk. 'Please, take a seat, make yourselves comfortable.' He settled himself behind the desk, opening the notes which lay in front of him but scarcely giving them a glance. He knew about the notes. It was

Sally he wanted to look at, and she looked well, he was pleased to see.

'Can I say something before you start?' Nick said, and he nodded.

'Of course.'

'It's about the other day. I hope you didn't think I was pulling rank or trying to get preferential treatment—'

Sam waved him aside. 'Don't be silly. I'm glad you came and found me, Nick. I always try to see staff myself if I possibly can, just as a matter of professional courtesy, but with the change-over from Will Parry you could easily have slipped through the net, so I'm glad you brought it to my attention. And anyway, if you can't help your colleagues, it's a pretty lousy system.'

He glanced down at the notes, checked the EDD, or estimated date of delivery, and looked up again at his patient. 'OK, Sally, you're thirty-six weeks this week, is that right?'

Sally nodded. 'Yes—thirty-seven weeks on Sunday. I've been monitored every fortnight, and it's down to weekly now—and I had the scans in London at twenty and twenty-eight weeks to check for congenital heart abnormalities.'

'And they were clear.'

'Yes.'

Sam ran his eye over the notes again, checking them for the umpteenth time, but he knew the contents by heart except for the new weight, blood pressure and urine test results which had been added today. All of them were fine. He shut the folder and sat back.

'OK, now, obviously I can't make you any guarantees, but your check a fortnight ago with Will Parry seems to have been fine, as were all the previous ones, and so far everything looks OK today. We're as certain as we can be from the ultrasound scans that the baby's heart is normal, and, from looking at your notes from that time, it seems highly likely that your little girl's heart defect was a tragic one-off developmental anomaly, and it's most unlikely to be repeated.'

Sally nodded, but there was a lingering worry in the back of her eyes that only the safe delivery of a normal, healthy baby would take away.

'Is there anything you want to ask me?' he prompted, but she shook her head.

'Nothing you can tell me without lying,' she said with a brave smile. 'I'll just have to wait and see, but it's getting harder. I mean, I know the baby's heart is probably fine, but—well, there are other things that can go wrong, and I can't help worrying about them. I just feel…' Her eyes filled. 'I don't know—threatened, somehow.'

Sam nodded slowly. 'I'm sure. It's understandable. Just hop up on the couch and let me have a look at you.'

He rubbed his hands together to warm them, then laid them gently on the firm swell of her pregnant abdomen. He could feel the curve of a little bottom hard up under her ribs, and as he pressed down on it, he could feel the head descending neatly into the pelvis.

The baby wriggled in protest, and he could feel its solid little heels tracking over the inside of Sally's uterus under his hand.

'It's going to be a footballer, we reckon,' Nick said, watching from the sidelines, and Sam threw him a smile.

'Certainly active and reactive. It's a good size for your dates, not too much fluid—everything feels absolutely text-book normal. Having many Braxton-Hick's contractions?'

She nodded. 'Constantly. I didn't really have them before, it was too early on.'

He felt the tightening of her uterus then, under his hands, and then after a few seconds it relaxed again. 'Is that typical?'

'Yes—they're like that all the time. Is that OK?'

'Fine. It's what I'd expect. The head isn't engaged yet, but it's going to drop soon, and that should ease the discomfort under your ribs—give you a bit more room to breathe.'

He helped her sit up, and went back behind his desk, jotting down a few remarks in her notes while she straightened her clothes and sorted herself out. Then he capped his pen and sat back.

'Right, go home, do nothing abnormal. Don't over-exert yourself, don't treat yourself like an invalid, just be sensible. If it feels OK, it probably is. You've got my numbers. Call me at any time, day or night—and I really mean that. I'll see you next week unless you decide to go into labour. If you do, I'll see you before—but don't worry. As I said, everything looks textbook normal, and there's no reason why it shouldn't be. The baby's perfectly big enough now to be viable, and I'm sure it'll come when it's ready.'

She nodded and stood up awkwardly, Nick helping her to her feet with gentle concern.

Sam looked away, suddenly stupidly jealous of this devoted couple on the threshold of a miracle. To make a baby in the normal way, to watch it grow, to see it born, to raise it—this was everyone's birthright, and yet it had eluded him and Crystal and countless others. It had eluded these two before as well, of course, and that made this time all the more special.

And it wasn't only the baby, he realised. It was the love they shared, this couple, the tenderness between them, the gentle banter as she rearranged her clothes and Nick put her shoes back on because, as she said, her feet seemed to have got further away.

'You go and relax now,' he said, conjuring up a smile and holding the door for them. 'I'll see you soon. Take care of each other.'

He watched them go, then closed the door of his office and slumped down at the desk, suddenly acutely aware of how lonely his life was, how devoid of any meaningful adult relationship.

It didn't have to be, of course, but that was even more terrifying than the loneliness.

Molly wanted to see him, to talk about last Friday, and he didn't know what the hell she was going to say. He just felt he wasn't going to like hearing it, and he didn't want to open that particular can of worms again in a hurry. It had taken him the entire weekend to get the lid back on, and now nearly a week later he wasn't sure how successful he'd been.

He still wasn't sleeping properly, and when he did, his dreams were full-on Technicolor and definitely X-rated. They were getting worse, the worms thrashing away against that insecure lid and doing their damnedest to escape.

And Molly, for sure, was going to rip the lid off again and, unless he was very much mistaken, tip the whole wretched mess out all over his carefully orchestrated life.

*   *   *

'Angie?'

'Molly, how lovely to hear from you! How are you?'

Molly laughed wryly. 'Confused. Are you around? I'd love to talk to you if you're not busy.'

Angie chuckled. 'I'm always busy, but I'm always ready for an excuse to stop. Want to meet for coffee? Or lunch?'

'Coffee would be good. I need to get back for Libby.'

'And I've got to pick Laura up at three-thirty, so why don't we do a light early lunch? We'll meet halfway—in Norwich?'

'That would be wonderful.'

They chose a venue with a car park, and an hour later Molly walked into the café and Angie's open arms.

Her friend hugged her and stood back, searching her face. 'You look good,' she announced, and Molly laughed.

'I don't know why. I'm not sleeping properly.'

'Man trouble?'

Trust Angie to cut right to the chase. 'Not exactly,' she said evasively, but that wasn't good enough.

Angie's eyes lit up with curiosity, and she steered Molly towards the counter. 'Come on, we'll get coffee and then you can tell me all.'

All? Molly wasn't sure about that, but Angie, as the mother of Molly's other surrogate child, was the one person in the world who would understand Sam's feelings as well as Molly's, and she wanted a bit of inside information before confronting him tomorrow. If that meant spilling her guts, well, she'd just have to do it.

They found an empty table by the window and Angie set the tray down, slid into the seat and leant forwards, her eyes still alive with curiosity.

'So—tell me all.'

Molly laughed again. 'You really go for the jugular, don't you?' she said ruefully, chasing froth round on her coffee with a spoon.

Angie's face was immediately contrite. 'I'm sorry, but you know me. I can't do small talk—not when there's big talk lurking in the wings, and this is big, isn't it?'

Molly nodded slowly. She took a sip of her coffee and propped her elbows on the table, nursing the cup while she groped for words. 'How much does it matter to Laura, having me in her life?'

Angie blinked, and sat back a little, her face puzzled. 'A lot—a huge amount.'

'Because she knows who I am.'

'Yes—but she would have to. Mothers talk to their daughters about their obstetric history. I can't do that—I'd have to lie to her or refuse to answer her questions, and I won't do that, so she had to know.'

'But would it matter if I wasn't here?' Molly persisted. 'If she'd never met me, or didn't know who I was? Would it matter to her?'

Angie stared at Molly thoughtfully. 'I really don't know,' she said slowly. 'Yes, I'm sure it would. She feels comfortable with you—safe. It's like the circle's completed. She has three parents—me, Doug and you. Of course you matter.'

Her brows drew together into a puzzled frown. 'Molly, why are you asking me this? What's it about?'

For a moment she didn't answer, then she took a steadying breath and prepared to open her heart. 'Jack,' she replied slowly, 'it's about Jack.'

Angie leant forward, her face suddenly concerned. 'Your other surrogate baby?'

Molly nodded again. 'I've met up with him—and his father. His mother's dead, and his father's working at the hospital.'

'Good grief. And I take it from what you've been asking me that Jack doesn't know anything about you?'

'No, not yet. That's nothing to do with me, really, and he's only just three. I'm just trying to come to terms with seeing him when I thought I never would, and I wondered if you'd ever wished I wasn't around in Laura's life.'

'Never,' Angie said firmly, and so emphatically that Molly knew it was from the heart. Her eyes filled, and she nodded.

'Thank you. I needed to know that.'

'So—have you seen Jack? Is he all right? And what about his father? Is that really awkward? I mean, is he difficult about you and Jack? I thought they didn't want you to see him.'

'Sam didn't mind, it was Crystal,' Molly explained. 'And Sam hasn't been awkward—just the opposite. He's been wonderful.' She hesitated. 'That's the trouble. There's this attraction…'

Angie's mouth rounded in a silent O. 'Does he want to have an affair with you?' she asked, the curiosity back in her eyes at this new turn.

Molly shrugged. 'I don't know. I hope so. I want one with him.'

Angie studied her thoughtfully for a moment. 'Are you sure?'

'Sure?'

'That it's not just about Jack? About getting closer to him?'

She shook her head. 'No. Absolutely not. This is about

us, me and Sam, nothing to do with Jack. My relationship with Jack is just a complication, and I don't want to compromise it. That's why I wanted your advice.'

Angie nodded slowly. 'OK. Well, I would say if it's what you want, then go for it. It just doesn't seem like you—but, still, it's about time. When did you last have an affair? Yonks ago, I'll bet—either that or you're dead discreet.'

Molly gave her coffee an unwarranted amount of attention. 'Angie, I don't do affairs. That's why I needed to talk to you.'

'Well, *I* don't do affairs!' Angie said in amazement, and then leant forwards and lowered her voice, belatedly conscious of all the other diners. 'So, anyway, how can I help you?' she murmured. 'I'm not sure I'm qualified to give advice.'

'Oh, you are, because it's Jack I'm worried about.'

'Jack?'

Molly nodded. 'I've never had an affair—Mick was my first and only love, so I don't know what it's like when things go wrong. I just feel—I need to stay friends with Sam, no matter what happens, to keep the lines of communication open between me and Jack. If he needs me, he should be able to see me, and I don't want our relationship compromised because his father and I have history.'

Angie eyed her assessingly. 'You realise, of course, that you've already condemned this relationship before it's even started?'

Molly gave a humourless laugh. 'I have, haven't I? I think he's still in love with Crystal.'

'And yet you think he'd have an affair with you?'

She nodded.

'Why?'

Her cheeks burned, and she looked down into the cold, unappealing froth on her coffee. The chocolate sprinkle was drying round the rim, and she dipped her finger in the liquid and rubbed it, loosening the residue.

'Molly? Why do you think you could end up having an affair?'

She sat back, rubbing the tip of her finger on her napkin and reluctantly meeting Angie's all-too-seeing eyes.

'He kissed me.'

'Just once?'

Just? Molly laughed softly under her breath. 'Just once,' she agreed. 'I thought the hall would catch fire.'

'Spontaneous human combustion,' Angie said thoughtfully, and smiled. 'Sounds interesting. I should go for it.'

'And Jack?'

'You'll work it out. All sorts of people have relationships in compartments in their lives. You don't have to be all things to each other and, anyway, if it goes wrong it shouldn't stop you seeing Jack. After all, divorced couples manage to sort out custody arrangements.'

'But they have rights. I have no rights.'

'So don't let the affair end if you don't want it to,' Angie said, and she made it sound so simple that Molly believed her.

'I have to let it start first,' she pointed out, but Angie just laughed.

'It doesn't sound as though that's going to be a problem—and if you want me to babysit, just ask.'

Molly met her eyes and smiled slowly. Excitement and anticipation were bubbling inside her. 'I might just do that,' she vowed.

*   *   *

'Can you babysit for me tomorrow afternoon?'

Debbie shoved the door of the dishwasher shut with her hip and nodded, rubbing her hands on a teatowel to dry them.

'Sure. Have you got to go to the hospital?'

Sam contemplated lying, then thought better of it. 'No. I'm meeting Molly,' he said, and then immediately regretted his honest streak as Debbie's face became a window on her curious and warm-hearted soul.

'It's just to sort out some things to do with Jack,' he said lamely, trying to distract her, but she wasn't that stupid.

'Yeah, right,' she said, and, dropping the teatowel into the washing-machine, she propped herself on the front of the Aga and gave him a searching, level look. 'It's time, you know.'

'What's time?' he asked, kicking himself for encouraging her and not telling her to go to hell.

'Time you had a woman in your life. You're lonely, Sam. You shouldn't be. You've got so much to offer, and Molly's lovely. You should go for it.'

'There is no "it",' he said, lying to himself now as well as Debbie, but she saw straight through him and snorted softly.

'If you say so. Your supper's in the bottom of the Aga— it's some leftover cottage pie from last night. Mark and I are off now to the pub, we'll see you later. Oh, what time tomorrow, by the way?'

'I said I'd be there at three.'

'OK.' She headed for the communicating door, pausing as she went through it. 'Just think about it, Sam. Don't close the door on it—not till you've seen what's on the other side.'

And she closed her door, the real door, leaving him alone on his side.

Was that what he'd do if he turned away from Molly? Shut himself in alone on his side? But what lay through that door?

He swallowed hard, fear wrestling with eager anticipation. Damn. Too many feelings, too much emotion.

Jack wandered through from the sitting room, Mark's and Debbie's cat draped over his shoulder like a limp rag, and looked up at his father.

'Want a video,' he said.

Sam nodded, too distracted to insist on the 'please'. 'OK. Let me get my supper and I'll come.'

He spent the evening with Jack, watching children's movies and contemplating the can of worms that lay in wait for him on the other side of that door, and wished he could see into the future.

If he could, of course, if he'd been able to, he wouldn't be here now with Jack.

Maybe it was just as well that some things remained unknown—but just now, he would have given almost anything for a glimpse into the future...

CHAPTER SIX

IT WAS three o'clock on Saturday afternoon, and Molly felt sick. Her palms were damp, and her heart was thrashing against her ribs.

What if Sam laughed at her? What if he just said a flat-out no?

What if he didn't?

Her heart lurched into her throat, and she closed her eyes and sat down abruptly at the kitchen table. She was being silly. She was thirty-three and, as Angie had said, it was about time.

The cake was cooling on a wire rack on the side, and the kitchen was fragrant with the smell of baking. The kettle had boiled, the pot was warming, and all she needed now was Sam.

She glanced up at the clock. Three-ten. He was late.

Or else he wasn't coming.

Disappointment coursed through her, and with wry honesty she laughed at herself.

'Either you want him or you don't,' she said out loud, just as a car swept onto her drive and pulled up under the kitchen window.

Their eyes met through the two sheets of glass, and for a moment they both sat there. Then, drawing a steadying breath, Molly got to her feet and went to the door, her legs like jelly.

He was there by the time she reached it, flowers in his hand, and his face was unusually serious.

He's nervous, she realised with sudden insight, and felt instantly better.

'Come in,' she said, and he stepped past her with a quick flicker of a smile that didn't reach his eyes.

She led him to the kitchen, then looked down at the white-knuckled grip he had on the flowers and smiled.

'Are they for me, or did you just want something to strangle?' she asked softly, and he gave a short huff of laughter and held them out to her.

'I'm sorry. My social skills are a bit rusty. That's just to say I'm sorry about last week. I was a pig.'

'No, you weren't. You were just...' Running scared? She shrugged, leaving the end of the sentence hanging in mid-air for him to finish how he would. 'And thank you for the flowers, they're lovely.'

She took them from his hand and put them in the sink in the utility room, filling it with water to give them a chance to recover before she arranged them.

'Sit down,' she said, waving at the table as she turned the kettle on again and emptied the now lukewarm water out of the teapot.

'Cake smells good,' he said, to fill the silence, and she threw him a smile over her shoulder.

'It's date and walnut.'

One eyebrow shot up. 'Really? That's a bit risky, lots of people hate it.'

'But you don't. It's your favourite.'

The eyebrow came down, joining the other in the centre in a puzzled pleat. 'Lord. You remembered.'

Sam looked astonished, and she busied herself with the teapot. She remembered everything about him—every word, every gesture, every look he'd ever given her. It was all engraved on her heart, next to the bit that said, Molly loves Sam, but he didn't need to know that.

'It wasn't hard to remember, it's my favourite, too,' she said, dismissing it lightly and scooping up the laden tray. 'Could you open the door for me?'

She took him through to the sitting room, tidied within an inch of its life in his honour, and, setting the tray down on the coffee-table, she positioned herself firmly in an armchair and waved at the sofa. 'Sit down and make yourself useful. You can cut the cake.'

They ate, they drank, and then finally the pot was drained and there was nothing left to do, nothing to hide behind, and Sam's patience seemed to come to an end.

He put his cup back on the tray, leant back and eyed her warily.

'Molly, what's this about?'

Oh, lord. The palms of her hands prickled and she scrubbed them discreetly against her jeans. There was no way to do this subtly. She wasn't into seduction and subterfuge, it wasn't her way—at least, not that she was aware of. She looked up and met his eyes, dredging up the last ounce of her courage.

'How do you feel about having an affair?'

Sam thought he was going to choke.

His eyes widened, and he let his breath out on a shocked huff of surprised laughter.

'Pardon?' he said, convinced he hadn't heard her right, but apparently he had, because Molly said it again, slowly and carefully, avoiding his eyes this time and with hot colour scalding her cheeks.

He was glad she wasn't looking at him, because his face was bound to be transparent. His feelings were so confused he couldn't work them out, and he sure as hell couldn't explain them to her. He couldn't explain them to himself—

but gradually, as the seconds ticked by, one emotion fought its way to the top.

Need.

Raw, naked and unashamed, it ripped through him, leaving him gasping.

'Molly, I—'

'I don't want an answer now,' she said quickly, cutting him off. 'Just think about it. It seems logical, really,' she went on in a reasonable voice totally at odds with the screaming of his body. 'I mean, we're both free, we're both lonely, and we get on well, don't we? I thought having someone to do things with—silly things, like going for a walk and not having to feed the ducks, and going to the theatre and seeing a real play instead of a pantomime—all sorts of things, well, it would be fun. Wouldn't it?'

His body was still screaming, but his mind was following her words, and there was something missing from them—something his body was going to be sorely disappointed in, if he was right.

'You said—affair?' he said carefully, not wanting to leave any room for doubt on that one.

Her eyes flew up and met his, wary and—good grief, shy?

'Yes.'

'Is that what you meant?' he asked, pursuing it relentlessly. 'A sexual relationship? As well as the theatre and walks and other stuff?'

Her cheeks coloured again softly, but she held his eyes, her chin coming up a fraction. 'Yes. If you want. We don't have to, obviously—I don't want you to feel under any pressure if you don't want to change things—but, yes, that's what I meant.'

'Right.'

Hell's teeth. He had to admire her courage. Any fool

could allow a situation to develop and run out of control. It took real guts to take that first deliberate step that could change a relationship so fundamentally.

And that worried him, when he thought beyond his first immediate physical reaction, because their relationship was already complicated.

'So—where does Jack fit in all this?' he asked, his common sense finally fighting free from the tentacles of lust to reassert itself in the nick of time.

'He doesn't,' she said emphatically. 'Jack's something totally separate. I want to see him, off and on, for the rest of my life, and ultimately I think I'd like him to know who I am, as Laura does—but that's nothing to do with this. This is about us—you and me, two adults struggling alone to bring up our children, sharing adult…'

She floundered to a halt, clearly casting around for the right word, and Sam was content to wait for her to find it. It saved him having to think of anything to say, and as the only thing that came to mind was '*Yes!*', procrastination seemed like a good idea.

'Things,' she said eventually.

Sam still didn't speak—not until he could trust himself not to be hasty. Instead he stared down the garden, watching as a bluetit pecked at the fruit on a crab-apple tree, quite unaware of a cat on the fence just feet away watching it intently.

Finally the bird flew away, and he looked up at Molly again, searching her face for any hidden motive, any private agenda she wasn't revealing.

Not that it would be hard to guess at. It was obvious that if she had any other motive, it would be connected with Jack, but for some reason he didn't really understand he believed her when she said it was nothing to do with his son.

He thought of the kiss they'd shared in the hall just feet away, and heat surged through him. It would be so easy to take her up on her offer—too easy. And what then?

Would she demand commitment? She deserved it, God knows, but he didn't do commitment, not any more. Not since Crystal.

'What's the catch?' he asked, without thinking, and pain flashed in her eyes, quickly concealed.

'There is no catch,' she said softly, and she sounded hurt that he could even think it. 'No strings, Sam. Just you and me, for as long as either of us want, having a bit of fun when it's mutually convenient.'

Perversely, he felt disappointed that she'd settle for so little, but it was all he'd want for himself, and maybe she was still in love with Mick's memory and just being realistic. After all, why shouldn't they have some fun? They both worked hard, and they deserved a break.

'Can I think about it?'

She nodded slowly. 'Of course. I want you to. I want it to be a reasoned decision, nothing hasty or ill-considered that either of us will regret later.'

Sam nearly laughed. Oh, he'd regret it—he'd regret it whatever his answer was, one way or another.

'More tea?' she was saying, but he needed to get away from her before he lost his head and said or did something else he'd regret.

'I don't think so. I ought to go. It's Debbie's day off, really, and I don't like to take advantage.'

'OK.'

She looked relieved, he thought, as she ushered him out to the hall. He hesitated at the door, wondering if he dared to kiss her goodbye, but before he could move she came up on tiptoe and brushed his cheek with her lips, taking the decision out of his hands.

'Go on. Go and think. I'll see you next week.'

She stepped back, carefully placing herself out of reach, and with a wry smile he let himself out and drove away without looking back.

Well, she'd asked him.

Molly slithered down the wall onto the hall floor, her heart pounding, her legs finally giving way. Heaven only knows what he'd thought, but at least he hadn't laughed at her. He'd probably gone away to work out how to say no without hurting her feelings, knowing him.

Or did she know him? She'd thought she did, at least a little, but now she wasn't sure. She was horribly afraid she'd made a mistake and screwed up their future relationship—in fact, he'd probably gone to take legal advice about keeping her away from Jack!

Phrases like 'unfit mother' and the like sprang to mind, and she had to tell herself not to be ridiculous.

She wasn't Jack's mother, anyway, so it was irrelevant.

She got up, dusted herself off and went into the sitting room, clearing away the debris of their tea and cake and needlessly eating another thick slice just to settle her nerves.

It didn't. It sat on them like a lead weight, and she spent the entire evening with horrendous heartburn. Go and think, she'd told him, and now she wondered how long he'd think.

Too long, whatever.

The thought did nothing for her indigestion.

Molly went in on Monday morning wondering if Sam would have an answer for her, but within minutes she was too busy to worry about her own personal life.

She took over the management of a labour from the

midwife who'd been on all night. Her patient was exhausted, and the midwife, Karen, handed over the notes with a tired sigh.

'She's making heavy weather of it. She's just ground to a halt, really, poor girl. I've been trying to get her to eat and drink to keep her blood sugar up, but she's been refusing everything but water for the last couple of hours and I'm frankly glad to hand her over to someone else. I'm bushed, and so's her poor husband. I wish you luck.'

Great, Molly thought. Just what she needed to start the week off—but perhaps it was. She glanced at the notes. It was Alice's first baby, and she had been in labour since the early hours of Sunday morning. Now she was fully dilated but her contractions were going off, and she was too tired to care.

Molly went in and introduced herself to the couple, and even a quick glance revealed how worn out Alice was.

'Come on, darling, have a little apple juice,' her husband was saying, but she just turned her head away.

'Tony, I can't. I just want to go home. Can't I go home? I'll come back tomorrow, I promise, but I'm just so tired…'

Molly rubbed Alice's hand comfortingly and perched on the edge of the bed.

'You need to drink something with sugar in it to boost your blood-sugar levels. You probably need to eat, really, but at this stage it's probably better if you don't.'

'This stage? What stage? I've been like this for hours!'

'That's what I mean,' Molly said gently. 'You're nearly there, but you aren't making any progress, and your baby's exhausted, too. We need to move things on for both your sakes so that we don't have to intervene.'

'Intervene?'

'I think she means do a Caesarian section,' Tony said, obviously a couple of steps ahead of his wife.

She rolled her eyes. 'So you're saying drink up, like a good girl, and I'll feel like pushing? I don't think so. Not in this lifetime.' Her laugh was wry and bitter, and Molly felt for her.

'You'll be surprised how much better you'll cope with a bit more energy.'

'I could eat chocolate,' she said after a moment.

Her husband laughed. 'You can always eat chocolate. I've never known a time when you couldn't manage chocolate.'

'Well, she can have some. That's fine. It'll boost her blood sugar.'

'Except I haven't got any.'

'Go down to the shop in the entrance,' Molly suggested, and he went, leaving her alone with Alice. She met the woman's tired eyes and smiled reassuringly. 'Rest for a little while, and when Tony gets back you can eat some of the chocolate, and then we'll see if we can get you going again.'

'And if not?'

Molly shrugged. 'I don't know. I'll talk to Mr Gregory, the consultant in charge of your care, and see what he thinks. He might just let you carry on, or he might want to use suction.'

'Suction? That's like forceps, isn't it? Does that hurt the baby?'

Molly shook her head. 'No, I don't think so. Not like the old forceps did, or the early suction cups. The cups now are silicone, and they're lovely and soft. They fit neatly over the top of the baby's head and just help to guide it and give a bit of added traction. It'll just give you a hand if you can't manage the last bit on your own, and it's better for you than a section, if we can avoid it.'

Alice nodded. 'OK. I'll try without, first, if the chocolate works—but I really am so tired…'

Tears filled her eyes, and Molly hugged her gently and settled her down against the pillows, tucking the covers round her shoulders to keep her warm. Poor thing.

Still, hopefully the chocolate would help, and if she could get Alice to wash it down with a bit of apple juice, they might be in business.

It was a vain hope. Molly kept a close eye on the labouring woman's temperature and blood pressure, and monitored the baby's heartbeat every contraction, but the contractions were getting so weak now it hardly registered with the baby.

Then, miraculously, they seemed to pick up, but Alice was too tired to help, and the baby's heartbeat began to dip.

Molly didn't like it. She'd given her long enough, and Alice's husband had half walked, half carried her round the ward a couple of times to see if gravity could assist, but to no avail.

She called Sam, and then, of course, she realised she'd have to see him, and she didn't feel in the least bit prepared for it. What if he was funny with her?

He wasn't. He walked onto the ward moments after she bleeped him and beckoned to her, and she slipped out of the delivery room and was confronted by the calm, quiet professional she'd grown to respect.

'Morning, Molly. What have you got for me?'

She looked up into his eyes, wondering if she'd see an answer there, but there was nothing. No clue, but nothing to fear, either. Just Sam. Relief flooded through her, and she got straight to the point.

'Ineffective labour—she's a primigravida, and she's really struggling. She's been wonderful, but she's been in labour since yesterday morning and she's exhausted. She's fully dilated and still having contractions, but they're losing strength and she needs help, Sam. She's never going to do this on her own.'

'Have you catheterised her?'

She shook her head. 'Not yet. I was waiting for you, but it was my next trick, to see if we can buy her a little more room. I think she's just got so tired she can't do the last bit. She's had a bit of a sugar boost and that's helped the strength of her contractions, but she's too far gone to do much. Anyway, the baby's struggling now—the last leak of amniotic fluid was stained with meconium and the heartbeat's fluctuating now with every contraction. I think she's run out of time.'

He nodded. 'OK, let's have a look, and if it's that straightforward, I'll do a little lift with the suction. Has she had an epidural?'

Molly shook her head. 'No. She's refused all pain relief, I gather. I certainly haven't given her any.'

Sam arched a brow. 'Could be tricky. What if she needs an episiotomy?'

'She doesn't want one.'

'Nobody ever does, but I take it she wants the baby?'

'Of course. She's too tired to be sensible. We'll just have to look after her, Sam. She hasn't had any sleep. I've been putting warm compresses on her perineum to relax it and encourage her contractions, so she might not need it.'

He nodded. 'OK. We'll do what we can. We may not need to interfere too much, if we can just use the vacuum to give her enough help so she can do it herself. Let's have a look.'

While Sam examined Alice and explained what they

were going to do, Molly prepared the catheter and then inserted it, draining Alice's bladder and removing a potential obstacle to the passage of the baby. It wasn't always easy to empty the bladder completely when in labour, and when the mother was as exhausted as Alice, every little bit of pelvic capacity they could buy her helped.

'Right, let's just watch her through a contraction and see how she gets on. Alice, I'd like you to sit up on your heels for me, and when you have a contraction, just rock forwards onto the headboard so you're on all fours but a bit upright, OK? That'll give you the help of gravity and should make it easier.'

With Molly supporting her on one side and her husband on the other, they held her in position, but her contraction was weak, and even pushing as hard as she could, the baby made virtually no progress.

'OK, this isn't going to work, I agree. There just isn't enough maternal impulsion,' Sam said, stepping back so they could ease Alice down onto her side. 'If you can prop her up a little, she can stay like that if someone can support that top leg. Alice, I'm going to help you get the baby out, OK? I'm going to use a suction cup on the baby's head, and when you push, I'm going to give a little pull, and see if we can't do this together, OK? But you're going to need to help me as much as you can, all right?'

Alice nodded, tears filling her eyes. 'I wanted to do it properly. I wanted to do it myself, without help.'

'Darling, you can't, you're knackered,' her husband said tiredly. 'Let them help you.'

She nodded again, all fight going out of her, and Molly and Sam exchanged glances. If she gave up completely, she'd need a Caesarian, and Molly didn't want that for her.

'Come on, Alice, have some more apple juice,' she coaxed. 'Just a little bit. Tony, see if you can get her to take a bit more. She's going to need more strength to do this, we can't do it all.'

Leaving him coaxing, pleading and exhorting his wife to take chocolate and apple juice, Molly helped Sam set up the vacuum extractor.

'I don't like doing this without at least a local and an episiotomy—'

'I'm not having an episiotomy,' Alice said drowsily, and Sam sighed under his breath.

'OK, Alice, but you're going to have to help me as much as you can. I'll leave it for now, but if I feel the baby's suffering, I may have to do it anyway. Can I give you a local anaesthetic in readiness, just in case?'

She shrugged. 'If you must.'

'I must,' he muttered, and, taking the syringe Molly handed him, he infiltrated the tissues carefully with the anaesthetic. 'Right,' he said, and without any further delay he slipped the soft suction cup over the baby's head, his face creasing in concentration as he struggled to position it blind.

'OK, that feels good. Let's give it a go. Next contraction, Alice, I want a real effort from you, please, if you can.'

She nodded, and with her husband and Molly cheer-leading and encouraging her, and Molly holding her leg, she pushed down as Sam gently pulled, and the baby slid down a little, the crown of its head appearing. With the next contraction the head was born, and with one final push the little body slipped out into Sam's waiting hands.

There was a second of breathless silence, then a sorry little wail came from the baby and they all started to breathe again. It wasn't a lusty cry, but it was a cry for all that, and the baby's colour improved immediately.

They laid her on Alice's now soft tummy, and Molly took Alice's hand and rested it on her daughter's back.

'You've got a beautiful little girl,' she told them with a smile, and Tony's face crumpled.

'Well done,' Sam said with feeling. 'That was a terrific effort, Alice. You're a clever girl.'

He stripped off his gloves, squeezed Molly's shoulder and backed towards the door. 'I have to go, I'm in the middle of a clinic. I'll be back later. Bleep me if there are any complications, but I don't think there will be. She did it herself in the end.'

Molly nodded and watched him go, and it was only as the door swung shut she realised she still didn't have an answer to that burning question…

Sam changed his white coat for a clean one, tossed the other one into a laundry basket in the clinic and headed back to his office. He had patients to see, backing up into the hereafter, and he really didn't have time to think about Molly, but he just couldn't get her out of his mind.

Her proposition had been on his mind since Saturday afternoon, and he was no nearer a sensible conclusion now than he had been then.

A patient came in when he called her, leaving her companion in the waiting room.

'Is that your partner? He's welcome to come in, too.'

She smiled and shook her head. 'No, he's not my partner, or the baby's father. He's just a friend. We're both single parents, and he gives me a hand. We do stuff together as well, go to the cinema, the pub—it's nice to have a companion sometimes, without having the strings of a relationship.'

Sam made some noncommittal reply, but it gave him food for thought. He missed adult company, even though he had Debbie and Mark around, but they were a couple, and watching them together made him feel, if anything, even more alone.

Maybe he should take Molly up on her suggestion, but with qualifications. He'd talk to her later, he resolved, and turned his attention back to his patient.

It was much later, after Jack was in bed and he'd procrastinated even further, before Sam had time to talk to her.

He didn't want to do it over the phone, but asking Debbie and Mark to listen out for Jack yet again seemed unfair and, anyway, they might have gone out.

He went to make himself a drink and found them both still in the kitchen, however, with paperwork spread out over the kitchen table and deep in conversation.

'Hi,' he said as he walked in, and Debbie looked up and smiled distractedly.

'Hi. Sorry, did you want the table? Only we were looking at this business plan, and it needs a big space, but we'll move if you like.'

'No, that's fine,' he said, waving dismissively. 'Help yourself.' He tipped his head on one side and eyed Debbie thoughtfully. 'Does this business plan mean I'm going to lose you?' he asked, and she laughed and straightened up.

'I doubt it. It's for Mark's tapestries. We just thought there must be a better way than selling designs to shops.'

Mark looked up and shrugged diffidently. 'I dunno—we thought about marketing kits. Advertising in the Sundays, home magazines, that sort of thing. What do you think?'

Sam walked over to them. 'May I?'

They nodded, and he ran his eye over the plan, noting the careful costings, the projected time span before profitability—they seemed to have taken it very logically and without excessive optimism, and for their sakes he hoped it worked. It deserved to. Mark was extraordinarily talented, and Debbie was highly organised. It could be a winning combination.

'Looks good. I hope it works for you. Before you get too busy with the marketing, though, you couldn't do me a favour, could you?'

They looked wary, and he grinned. 'I'd like to pop out for a while—will you be in if I leave Jack?'

Their faces eased, and Mark's eyebrow went up, the ring in it catching the light and giving him a faintly piratical air. 'Molly?' he asked, and Sam felt the colour rise on the back of his neck. Was nothing private round here?

'Just one or two things of Jack's I wanted to show her—from the early days. I forgot to take them the other day.'

'You don't have to make excuses, mate,' Mark said, a grin spreading over his face. 'You go for it—she's a real cracker.'

Et tu, Brute? They all seemed in a hell of a hurry to get him involved with a woman again—to free them to develop the business? Who could tell?

He didn't pause to ring her. She might have been out, but it was a risk he was prepared to take. And, of course, when he arrived there was another car on the drive, and she had visitors.

Damn. He'd turned into her drive, of course, and his headlights had swung across and caught her attention, and she was standing at the kitchen window now, looking out at him. He could hardly drive off without talking to her, and yet this conversation wasn't one he wanted to have in a hurried way or on the doorstep, with strangers hanging on their every word.

She'd left the window and he contemplated running, but then the front door opened and she came out, hugging her upper arms against the chill of the evening, and he was trapped.

He turned off the engine and got out, walking over to her, still not knowing quite what to say.

'Come on in,' she invited. 'Mick's parents are here. Come and meet them.'

The Hammonds were the last people in the world he wanted to meet, bearing in mind what he was going to say to their daughter-in-law, but he went anyway, and they were lovely—friendly, interested in Jack's progress. And when Molly turned to them and asked if they'd mind keeping an eye on Libby for an hour while she slipped out, they didn't turn a hair.

Good grief, he thought, don't tell me they're in on it. But that was stretching his imagination a little too far.

She shrugged into a light jacket, picked up her bag and smiled her thanks at them. 'You've got my mobile number. We won't be far away—we'll just go for a quick drink.'

'You take your time. It's nice to see you getting out a bit,' Mick's father said, and Sam wondered if he'd be quite so magnanimous if he knew what his daughter-in-law had proposed—and what Sam's response was going to be!

They took his car and drove out into the nearest village, finding themselves a quiet table in the corner of the bar. Neither of them were drinking, and Sam regretted his scruples about drink driving. A hefty slug or two of whisky would help this conversation along a treat, he thought.

'I'm sorry to break up your evening,' he began, but she laughed.

'Don't be silly. I'd much rather be with you. They're dear, sweet people, but we're not exactly on the same wavelength.'

Well, that allayed his fears about what she might have told them, anyway!

'So,' she said, finally breaking the silence that was stretching between them like over-stressed elastic, 'I take it you wanted to talk to me?'

He set down his glass with needless precision, centring it exactly on the beer mat, lining up the edge of the mat with the table—anything to avoid taking that next, terrifying step.

Her voice cut into his whirling thoughts. 'Is it no? I can take it, Sam. Just tell me.'

Leave it to Molly to make it easier. He looked up and smiled wryly. 'No, it's not no. It's not yes, either—not exactly. I mean—can we try the theatre thing first? We can't turn the clock back, and I don't want us to do anything hasty that might turn out to be wrong for either of us.'

Sam fiddled with the mat again, pushing it so it was diagonally across the corner, adjusting it by microns. Finally he started speaking again, the carefully rehearsed words sounding stiff and awkward in his head. He abandoned them, going instead with his feelings, letting his heart talk.

'I know you don't do this sort of thing lightly, and the fact that you asked me—well, I was going to use words like privileged and honoured, but they just sound patronising, and I don't mean to. I don't want you to think I don't want you, Molly—you must know I do. Hell, I make it obvious enough. It's just—can we take it one step at a time? See how it goes? It would be too easy just to go to bed with you and take what you're offering, and I don't want to do that. You're too important to me, and I respect you far too much to do that.'

She smiled, her eyes filling. 'You are silly. I wouldn't think you didn't respect me.'

'I just don't want to rush it.'

'Fine. We won't. We'll start now, with a drink, and we'll go from there. OK?'

He felt the tension seep out of him like a perished balloon, and he laughed softly and lifted his glass to her. 'Good idea—except I have to get back. I'm intruding on Mark and Debbie's time again.'

Molly withdrew a fraction, her smile becoming fixed. 'Oh, well. Another time.'

'Thursday? There's a new film out I'd like to see. I thought maybe we could have a meal as well—if you can get a sitter. I'm sorry it's midweek, but Debbie and Mark have the weekend off, and Friday's sacrosanct for them.'

Her eyes softened, and he realised she'd thought he was brushing her off, letting her down gently.

Like hell.

'That would be lovely,' she said, the smile lighting her eyes, and Sam wondered how he was going to keep his hands off her until then.

He didn't, in fact. He drove her home, and just before they reached the streetlights in her road, while they were still in the rich velvet darkness of the countryside, he pulled in to the side of the road and drew her into his arms.

'This is just a goodnight kiss, in private,' he said, his voice threaded with tension again. As she melted against him, he lowered his mouth to hers.

She tasted glorious. He wanted to lose himself in her, and it took all the strength he had to release her and ease away, sitting up with his arms wrapped round the top of the steering-wheel and his forehead resting against his white knuckles.

'Sam?'

Turning the key, he lifted his head and turned towards

her, studying her in the dim light of the instrument panel.
'Yes?'

'Thank you.'

His laugh was harsh and cynical. 'Don't thank me. I
was this close—'

'Me, too. That's why I'm thanking you.'

One step at a time, he reminded himself. Pulling out
onto the road again, he took her home.

CHAPTER SEVEN

WELL, Molly thought.

It was a start—and what a start, if that goodnight kiss was anything to go by. Sam might be taking it one step at a time, but he had a long stride! Humming softly to herself, she went upstairs, checked on Libby and ran herself a bath.

The Hammonds had gone home, gently curious but not pushy—never pushy. Unlike Mick, they were prepared to give things time. He'd always been impatient—a bit like Sam, really.

How interesting. She'd never thought of them like that before, but she supposed in many ways they were alike.

She eased herself into the hot water, her brow pleating into a little furrow as she considered that extraordinary fact. Sam and Mick, as different as chalk and cheese and yet with the same essential qualities of decency and loyalty and human-kindness.

Not to mention impatience and a terrible tendency not to talk about things. Mick had been reluctant to talk to her at first, but then they'd reached a turning point in their relationship, and he'd opened up to her and given her everything.

Would Sam ever do the same—and if he did, would he say what she wanted to hear?

She was rather afraid not.

Oh, rats. She must give up this stupid habit of trying to second-guess everything, and just give events time to work themselves out. Refusing to think any more about that kiss or the possible consequences of it, she slid under the water, coming up gasping with her hair streaming in wet ribbons over her shoulders.

Sam would keep. Just for now she had to get bathed, dry her hair and get to bed, because she was on an early tomorrow and time was pressing on.

And in the afternoon, she'd go and see her GP and get herself put on the Pill.

Just to be on the safe side.

Thursday came before he was ready for it. Sam had spent the entire week alternately regretting the kiss and looking forward to the next one, and suddenly it was Thursday evening and he was taking Molly to the cinema.

He'd seen Nick and Sally Baker in his clinic that afternoon, and unless he was mistaken Sally was about to go into labour—which was all very well, but he really, *really* didn't want them to ring him tonight!

He put his phone on silent and slid it into his trouser pocket, so he'd feel it vibrate if they called him, and pulled up on Molly's drive five minutes early.

Looking keen, he thought in disgust, and decided it was better than looking indifferent and being rude.

Whatever, she was ready and came straight out, looking better than a woman of thirty-three with three kids under her belt had any right to look, and he was suddenly glad they were going to the cinema and it would be dark.

The film he'd wanted to see, however, was full when they arrived, and he kicked himself for not booking in advance. Lord, he really was losing his grip. Molly, however, didn't seem to mind at all.

'I didn't really fancy it that much anyway,' she confessed, wrinkling her nose and filling him with an overwhelming urge to kiss the tip. Idiot. She was pointing at the display behind the cashier. 'How about that?' she suggested instead.

'That' turned out to be a romantic comedy, and its silly tenderness made him want to laugh and cry and hug her—preferably while he had her in his arms in a great big bed somewhere miles from anywhere. Much less thought-provoking than the film he'd intended them to see, and with quite the opposite effect, of course. Once again he was grateful for the darkness.

They'd decided not to do dinner, because Debbie and Mark were both feeling a little off colour, so when he turned into her drive after the film it was still quite early.

'Would you like to come in?' she asked, and he nearly agreed, but Libby was staying with her grandparents and so their chaperone was missing. Not a good idea, he decided. The likelihood of him disgracing himself was so high it didn't bear thinking about, especially after that silly, tender film—and, anyway, he couldn't get out of the car or she'd be only too aware of his feelings.

'I shouldn't,' he said. 'I've got work to do, really.'

Not a lie, but not the truth, either. Oh, hell. A shadow fell over Molly's face, and he wasn't sure if it was a trick of the light or if she was disappointed. Damn. Maybe he should go in and to hell with the consequences…

'Right,' she said quietly. 'Well, thanks for a lovely night. I really enjoyed the film. I'll see you tomorrow?'

'Sure.'

She opened the door and got out, and on impulse Sam leant over and looked up at her as she was about to close it again.

'Molly? What are you doing on Sunday morning? I know you said you'd like to go for a walk without feeding the ducks, but you also want to see Jack. The trouble is, if we go anywhere near the park Jack will insist on feeding the ducks, but I would guess Libby's much too old and sophisticated to do that now.'

She laughed, a lovely sound that rippled over his nerve-endings, and he saw the light come back into her eyes. 'Libby loves the ducks. If I contrive a whole loaf of stale bread as an excuse, I'm sure she'll manage to deal with her pride.'

'Fine. Do you want to meet us there, or shall I pick you up?'

'We'll meet you there—unless it's raining. If it's raining we'll have to think of something dry to do.'

'I'll work on it. I'll see you tomorrow morning—are you on early?'

'Yes, for my sins. That's why the Hammonds have got Libby.'

'Look out for Sally Baker—Nick's wife—A and E consultant?'

'Yes, I know them both. Sally's a nurse. Heavens, is she due already?'

'Just about. She's around thirty-eight weeks. I don't know if you're aware of it, but she lost a baby some years ago with a heart condition, and she's fretting, even though this one seems absolutely spot on. She'll need TLC—and I want to know if she turns up. I saw her earlier today and I have a feeling she's imminent.'

'OK. I'll look out for her. I'll see you tomorrow—and thanks again. I really enjoyed it.'

'Me, too. Take care. Sleep well.'

'You, too.' She smiled, her face softening, and closed the door, and the moment she was inside the house he put the car into reverse and turned it round, shooting off down the road in a squeal of tyres and growling with frustration.

Why had he had to tell her to sleep well? The last thing he needed to think about was her lying in bed, those soft brown curls spread out on her pillow, her body warm and relaxed in sleep.

Until he touched her…

Sam gave a low growl and slowed for a roundabout, gunning away from it with another immature display of testosterone.

Despite his parting remark, Molly didn't sleep well. That silly film had left her even more aware of her loneliness and the yawning void in her emotions that only Sam could fill. If he'd come in…

If he'd come in, she told herself sternly as she showered for work, she would have thrown herself at him, and made a complete fool of herself. He clearly wasn't interested in taking their relationship that far, even if he did respond to her. It was just automatic. He was a man. It was like breathing to them—woman equals sexual reaction.

Oh, rats.

She arrived on the ward to find that Sally Baker had been admitted at five a.m. She went into the labour room and met Sue in the doorway.

'Oh, hi. I was just coming to look for you before you got embroiled somewhere else. Mr Gregory wants you to look after Sally.'

'I know, that's fine. How are things?'

'Fine. Great. Good, steady progress. She was four centimetres dilated at six—I haven't checked her since but I would think she's about five or six now. Good, strong contractions every five minutes, but I think the interval's closing now and she's going to hot up.'

'Pain relief?'

Sue shook her head and lowered her voice. 'She doesn't want anything that might affect the baby—she's got history. You need to look at the notes.'

'Sam filled me in briefly.'

'OK. She's managing well—she's got a good coach. Do you know Nick?'

Molly nodded, smiling at him over Sue's shoulder. 'We've met, down in A and E. Hello, Sally.'

'Molly? Hi. Are you going to look after me?'

'For my sins,' she said with a smile.

'They're both in the profession, of course, so they'll keep you on your toes,' Sue said, loud enough for them all to hear, then turned back to Sally and Nick with a grin. 'Right, Sally, I'm going to leave you in Molly's capable hands. I hope you have a really great day, and I'll come and see you and the baby tonight, OK?'

'OK.' Sally's smile was faint, just a polite social smile, and Molly could see the fear behind it. Poor girl. Still, from what Sam had said she had no need to worry, but that wouldn't stop her, and to reassure her Molly would be monitoring her very closely.

She smiled at them, going over to Sally and rubbing her shoulder gently. 'Hello, my love. How are you doing? I gather from Sue that you've got a really good coach here.'

Sally gave another faint smile that didn't reach her eyes. 'Yes, he's great. It's OK so far—or it was. Oh, rats. Nick?'

He moved closer, rubbing her back gently through the contraction, his attention focused totally on his wife. When it was over he straightened up and met Sally's eyes and smiled.

'OK now?'

She nodded.

Molly checked her watch again, timing the length of the contraction and making a mental note. 'Right, the first thing I want to do is check your obs, then I'll examine you and see how much progress you've made in the last hour and a half, and we'll go from there. Are you feeling more comfortable now?'

'I'm all right.'

'Have you had breakfast?' she asked as she took Sally's temperature, but she shook her head.

'She won't eat,' Nick said gruffly.

'What about you?' Molly asked him, checking Sally's pulse, her eyes flicking across to take in his strained eyes and rumpled hair. He didn't look a lot better than his wife, she thought.

'No, I haven't had anything.'

'Well, I think you both should—especially you, Nick. We don't want you keeling over, you're much too big to catch. Why don't you go and—'

'I don't want him leaving me,' Sally said, reaching out to him.

'I'm not going anywhere, darling.'

'Yes, you are. You're going to stick your head out of the door and ask a passing HCA to rustle up some tea and toast, some apple juice and a pot of honey.'

Nick's face relaxed a little. 'OK. Now you've started talking about it, I'm absolutely starving.'

'And you, young lady, are going to eat something too,' Molly said firmly but kindly. 'Right, your obs are fine. Let's have a listen to this baby.'

'Can't I have a foetal heart monitor on?' she asked, and Molly looked at the fear in her eyes and hugged her.

'Of course you can, if you want, but I'm sure there's really no need, and they're quite restricting. Let's just listen with the Sonicaid for now.'

She picked up the baby's heartbeat instantly, strong and regular and as steady as a rock, and Sally's whole body relaxed.

Not for long. She had another contraction, the second

since Molly had come in, and checking her watch Sally saw that it was just over three minutes since the last. Sue was right, Sally was hotting up.

Molly washed her hands, snapped on a pair of gloves and checked the progress of Sally's cervix with deft, gentle fingers.

'You're doing well,' she said with a smile as Sally relaxed again after yet another contraction. 'Six to seven centimetres. Right, I think we need to get a little food into you if you think you can eat, but certainly apple juice for the sugar boost.'

Sally nodded. 'So—how long will it be?' she asked, and for the first time Molly saw a thread of hope and excitement in amongst the fear.

'I don't know. One to three hours, at a guess, but I can't tell. It might be less.'

She chewed her lip for a moment, then looked up at Nick who was hovering in the doorway, still waiting to catch someone's attention to ask for the food.

'Nick, go and find someone. I'll be all right if you're on the ward.'

'You sure?'

'Of course I'm sure.'

With one last backward glance Nick left them alone, and Sally looked up at Molly with worried eyes. 'I'm so scared,' she confessed. 'I really wanted this baby, but my whole pregnancy's been a nightmare of worry. They keep telling me everything's all right, but I don't dare to believe it. Do you think I'm mad?'

Molly shook her head. 'No. I think it's perfectly understandable. You've had a terrible experience and it's been very damaging. Of course you're frightened, but everything looks wonderful so far, and the best thing you can do for this baby is relax as much as possible. It'll soon be over.'

'Not soon enough.'

'It really won't be long,' Molly said gently. 'When you're holding your baby in your arms, this will all seem like a bad dream.'

'I know the heart's all right,' Sally said, twisting her hands together. 'It's all the other things that can go wrong. Sometimes I wish I wasn't a nurse. Have you had any children?'

'Three.'

'I bet they're a real handful.'

Molly smiled wistfully. 'Well, Libby can be, but the other two aren't mine—I was a host surrogate mother for them, so other people have the joy of struggling with them.'

Sally's eyes widened. 'How on earth could you go through all this and give them away?' she asked, stunned.

Molly shrugged. 'I wanted to help other people. Libby gave us so much joy. I wanted to share that.'

'And doesn't it hurt you?'

She shrugged again. 'Sometimes, of course, but not really. I see them both, they're lovely, happy children—I've got no regrets.'

'Good lord, I think you're amazing. It took Nick nearly a year to talk me into this, but he wasn't there when I lost the other one. We—weren't together at the time. We'd lost touch, and I didn't see him again for seven years. He didn't really know what it was like—or, at least, I didn't think he did, but I think now he's more worried than I am.'

Molly squeezed her hand. 'I wish I could reassure you. You know the statistics, though, I'm sure. The chances of anything going wrong at this stage in a normal, healthy pregnancy are very slight, and I'm watching you like a hawk, anyway. But you just won't believe me, will you, till you're holding your baby?'

Sally gave a hollow laugh. 'Sorry. I know you're right. It's just—'

'Hey, presto! Breakfast!'

Nick came in brandishing a tray, and Sally took one look at the contents, sniffed the air slightly and went green.

'Oh, no, I'm going to be sick,' she said, and promptly followed through, leaving Nick looking shocked and riddled with guilt.

'Just take the tray out,' Molly advised with a smile, cleaning Sally up with practised hands. 'Eat something while you're out there. You can come back in with the apple juice in a minute.'

'I'm having a contraction,' Sally said, her eyes widening and searching frantically for Nick.

'It's OK, I'm here. Roll on your side towards me,' Molly said firmly. 'Now just flop. Let all the tension go, and breathe nice and light up here, in the top of your chest—that's lovely. Well done. Good girl. That's brilliant.'

Her hand was rubbing gently over Sally's back as she spoke, and she could feel the tension drain out of her as the contraction passed. 'Good girl. Well done. It's all over.'

'For a minute.'

'They are getting closer. I think you're moving into transition.'

'I'm not moving anywhere,' Sally said, a trace of truculence in her voice.

Molly chuckled. 'That's fine. You can have your baby here, there's no problem with that. I'll just get Sam Gregory, though. He'll be cross with me if he misses it.'

Had he been listening outside? Whatever, as she voiced

the thought he came in with Nick at his side, and his eyes flicked to Molly for a quick update, one eyebrow arched in enquiry.

'I think she's in transition.'

He nodded briefly, and smiled at Sally. 'Hi, there. You're doing well, I gather. Molly, have you checked her cervix recently?'

'Not since seven-thirty.'

Sam checked the clock on the wall. It was nearly nine. 'Time to do it again?'

'Want to do the honours?' she offered, but he laughed softly and shook his head.

'I'm not a midwife. You'll do it better.'

She chuckled in surprise. 'Such high praise—or are you saving yourself for the dramatic stuff?' she teased as she examined Sally. 'If so, I'm going to have to disappoint you. She's fully dilated and ready to go, and everything's hunky-dory.'

'That's fine, I'll sit back and watch the proceedings. I could do with a lazy morning, having been dragged out of bed at something after four because someone decided to go into labour in the middle of the night.'

Molly looked at him in surprise. 'Have you been here since then?'

'Yes—why? You sound shocked.'

She laughed. 'Well, not shocked, exactly, but I would have thought you'd be in here making your presence felt before now.'

'What—annoying the midwife?' he ribbed. 'More than my life's worth. I know my place, I come when I'm called.'

'I'm glad someone does,' Sally offered with a pointed look at her husband. 'Most consultants make it their job to interfere with the nursing staff.'

'And vice versa—which, of course, is how you got yourself in this mess,' Nick teased, and Sally laughed weakly.

'I didn't mean that kind of interference,' she said, and then the smile vanished from her face and a look of intense concentration came over it. 'Oh, help, I want to push. I want to get up. Nick? I want to kneel. I want—'

'Want, want, want,' Nick said, but despite the teasing note in his voice his eyes were troubled. The end was close, and any minute now they'd know if their baby was all right.

'Sally, pant for me,' Molly instructed a few minutes later, crouching down behind her as she hung on to the head of the bed with Nick supporting her. 'Don't push any more, you're nearly there, just let it come slowly—that's lovely. Well done, the head's here—and the rest. Well done!'

The baby's cry was strong and immediate, and Sally turned round and collapsed down onto the pillows, tears streaming down her cheeks.

'Oh, he's lovely. It's a boy, he's gorgeous! Oh, hello, baby,' she said softly, reaching out to hold him as Molly laid him on her now soft tummy. 'Oh, Nick…'

Nick couldn't speak. The tears were flooding his eyes, and he sat down beside her, wrapped her and the baby in his arms and just held them.

Molly turned away, giving them a moment of privacy, and met Sam's bleak eyes. He smiled, but the smile was strained and he turned away.

'Well, that's excellent. I'll check him in a minute. Apgar score?'

'Ten, from what I can tell. He's lovely—he reminds me of Jack.' Her voice cracked, and she stripped off her gloves and washed her hands, then checked the baby again, cov-

ering him once more in a warmed towel and helping Sally
to put him to the breast.

'He is OK, isn't he?' Sally said worriedly, and Molly
smiled and nodded.

'He seems fine—gorgeous. We'll get a paediatrician
down to check him now, though, just to set your minds at
rest. Apgar ten at five minutes,' she murmured to Sam,
turning her head, but he wasn't there. He'd slipped silently
from the room while she'd been busy, and she wanted to
go after him, but she couldn't leave them, not at this stage.

But those bleak eyes haunted her, even after Sam came
back in a few minutes later with some excuse about calling
the paediatrician, and his eyes were just his eyes again,
filled with gentle smiles and teasing humour and reassur-
ance for the blissful family in his care.

So what had put that look there?

Jealousy? Was Sam jealous of Nick and Sally and their
happiness? She could understand that. There were times—
like this—when other people's happiness just underlined
the emptiness of her life. Did Sam feel like that, too?

And if so, would he turn to her in the end to fill that
void in his life? She could only hope.

Sam smiled and chatted and cuddled little baby Baker du-
tifully, and all the time he just wanted to get the hell out
of there, away from so much love and happiness.

Molly was giving him strange, assessing looks, and he
was glad when Josh Lancaster came down and he could
leave them all with the paediatrician and make his escape,
promising to come back and see them all later.

It was getting a little crowded in there, anyway, with a
continuous stream of visitors from A and E, and they
hardly noticed he'd gone.

All except Molly, of course. She caught his eye as he

slipped out, and the searching look she gave him was the last straw. He left the department, going down to the clinic and apologising to his registrar for abandoning him with all the patients. Within minutes he was up to his eyes again, and the Bakers, for the time being, were pushed to the back of his mind.

Sunday was a gorgeous day. The autumn tints were just starting to touch some of the trees in the park, and Molly found herself racing Libby down a grassy hill towards the duck pond. She tripped at the bottom, Libby cannoning into her, and they ended up in a tangled, giggling heap at the edge of the path.

'Such unseemly behaviour.'

Suddenly conscious of what an idiot she must look, she tipped her head back and looked up into Sam's laughing eyes.

'Well, hello there,' she said, still breathless, and scrambled to her feet, brushing grass and leaves off her clothes and helping Libby up with the other hand. 'Hello, Jack. Fancy seeing you here.'

Jack looked at her as if she'd come from outer space. 'Hello, Molly,' he said, and looked up the hill. 'Me run like Libby.'

'I don't think that's a good idea,' Sam said. 'And anyway, the ducks are waiting. They'll want their breakfast.'

'We're going to feed the ducks, too,' Libby said, looking pleased that they'd got company. 'Mum forgot we'd got fresh bread and took a loaf out of the freezer yesterday, so we've got tons. We haven't fed the ducks for ages. Shall we go and find them, Jack?'

She took his hand in hers and set off with him along the path, Sam staring worriedly after them.

'It's fine, she knows where to go, she's fed the ducks here for years with Mick's parents.'

He threw her a rueful smile. 'Sorry. There are just so many nasty people about.'

'I don't think there are, we just hear about them now, but I know what you mean. Don't worry, we'll soon catch them up.'

They followed them down the path, keeping them easily in sight, and as they started walking Molly winced a little.

'Are you OK?'

She laughed. 'Just too old to throw myself down hills,' she confessed. 'It seemed like a good idea at the time.'

'You looked as if you were having fun.'

'We were.' She shot him a searching look. 'Sam, are you OK?'

His stride faltered for a second. 'Of course. Why?' He managed to sound puzzled, but Molly wasn't fooled.

'Oh, the other day,' she said calmly. 'With the Bakers. You seemed a bit—I don't know. Unhappy.'

'Just thoughtful. I'd come from the clinic. There was another couple there who aren't going to have such a happy outcome. It just brought it home a bit.'

How plausible. Funny that she didn't believe a word of it, but if he didn't want to tell her the truth, she could hardly make him. She held up her bag, changing the subject. 'I've got the bread—we'd better catch them up,' she said, and hurried after the children, leaving Sam to follow in his own time.

They'd just reached the fenced edge of the pond when Molly caught up with them. She handed Libby the bag of bread and watched as her daughter tore up the bread and handed it to Jack, a piece at a time, and helped him throw it to the waiting ducks.

'You shouldn't really give them bread,' Sam murmured

in her ear, and she turned to reply and found him just inches away.

They froze, and his eyes tracked to her mouth and then slowly, feature by feature, traced her face and returned to her eyes. Heat blazed in his eyes and, swallowing hard, he stepped back a fraction and the tension eased.

'Yes,' she said inanely. 'I know. It pollutes the water.'

'And gives them too much refined grain and salt. They don't need salt.'

I can't believe we're talking about the ducks, she thought almost hysterically. He was *that* close to kissing me...

'Jack, no, don't put your fingers through the bars, that's a good boy.'

The spell was broken, and Molly moved away from Sam, giving him room to get to his son while she took the bread bag from Libby and ripped up some of the slices. Anything to vent her frustration!

'Feel sick,' Jack said suddenly, and there was a retching, splashing noise and Libby leapt out of the way with a shriek.

'Oh, Mummy, my shoes!' she wailed, and Jack started to cry.

So much for that little outing, she thought, and sighed. 'Go and wipe them on the grass, darling. Sam, is he OK?'

Sam was crouching down, wiping Jack's mouth with a tissue and scanning his face worriedly.

'I don't know. He feels a bit clammy. I think I'll take him home. Is Libby all right? I'm sorry about her shoes.'

'Don't worry, they'll be fine. They'll wash. Ring me later, let me know how he is.'

'Will do.'

She watched him go, then went over to Libby and helped her clean up her shoes.

'Oh, Mummy, they stink. I don't know how you can be a nurse.'

'I'm not a nurse, I'm a midwife, but you just get used to it. Shall we go home and change your shoes and do something else?'

Libby nodded, and they returned to the car, putting the offending shoes in the boot for the journey home, arriving back in the nick of time before a sudden squally rainstorm. It was the end of the nice weather that day, and they spent the rest of the day pottering about in the kitchen and making cookies, and then Molly cleared up while Libby did her violin practice.

She was getting better, Molly thought with pride, and wondered what her father would have made of her. He would have adored her, she knew. She'd been the apple of his eye, and he would have given anything to watch her grow up.

Sudden foolish tears stung Molly's eyes, and she brushed them away angrily. This was all because of Nick and Sally Baker and their lovely baby. All that abundant joy was a bit much to take, and knowing how richly they deserved it did nothing to stop the emptiness inside.

She made some sandwiches, put the cookies on a plate and made a pot of tea, then went through to the sitting room.

'Time to stop,' she told Libby. 'The cookies are cool enough to eat now—although I notice there weren't quite as many as I thought we'd made.'

Libby giggled guiltily and put her violin down, kneeling on the floor on the other side of the coffee-table and taking a sandwich, peering inside it inquisitively.

'Tuna,' Molly told her, and Libby sank her teeth into it and sighed.

'Yum. I was hungry. Lunch seems hours ago.'

'Lunch *was* hours ago. You've been practising for an hour, and it took us ages to make the cookies.'

'Can I have one?'

'No. Sandwiches first,' she said, 'and then, if you're very lucky and I leave you any, you can have one.'

'One?' Libby wailed, and Molly laughed and relented.

'All right, more than one,' she conceded, and, curling her feet up under her bottom, she settled back in the corner of the sofa and watched her daughter.

CHAPTER EIGHT

THEY watched television together that evening, and then Libby went to bed, leaving Molly alone with the rest of the evening stretching away ahead of her like a prison sentence. She curled up with a book, but neither it nor the television could hold her attention, and in the end she went to bed at half past nine.

The phone rang at ten to ten, just as she put her light out, and it was Sam.

'Jack's a bit better,' he said. 'I'm sorry I'm ringing you so late, but he's been really grotty all day. He's just gone to sleep now. He hasn't been sick for hours, but Debbie tells me there was a bug at playgroup. How are Libby's shoes?'

Oh, lord. 'Still in the car,' she said, contemplating getting up and going outside in the rain to fetch them and clean them up ready for the morning. Oh, well, Libby could wear her others. 'I hope you get a decent night's sleep.'

'I think I will now,' he said, and he sounded weary enough. Molly could empathise. She'd been through it with Libby several times, and knew just how wearing a sick preschooler could be.

By the morning, she had a fair idea of what a nearly-ten-year-old could be like. At six-thirty she phoned the hospital to say she couldn't come in until later, and at eight she called the Hammonds and asked them if they could help.

They came over immediately, and she arrived on the ward just as Sam came down from Theatre.

'Hi—you look harassed. Is everything all right?' he asked, and she laughed.

'Sort of. It seems to be catching. Libby's been up most of the night.'

'So've I,' he said, and she noticed the lines around his mouth. 'You'd better go home. You're bound to get it, and we don't really need it on the ward. It's short and sharp and vile, but at least it's over quickly.'

He wasn't wrong. It only took five hours to work its way through her system, but in that time she could quite cheerfully have died.

Molly went back to work the following day feeling almost one hundred per cent, and found several of her colleagues had been struck down with the bug. She was rushed off her feet for the next two days, and hardly saw Sam.

When she did it was Thursday morning, and he caught up with her just outside the ward.

'Molly.'

She went over to him, wondering what he wanted, but one look in his eyes proved it was nothing to do with work.

'Tomorrow night—it's really short notice, but is there any chance you could get a babysitter? Mark and Debbie are away for the weekend and they're taking Jack down with them and leaving him with Crystal's parents for a few days—I'm picking him up on Wednesday. I just thought, if you could get someone to look after Libby...'

She tried not to grin inanely. 'Libby's with my parents for the weekend,' she told him. 'I'm working on Saturday morning, so they're coming to pick her up tomorrow afternoon after school and keeping her until Sunday night.'

Something flared in Sam's eyes and was quickly controlled, but an answering flame shot through her. 'What did you have in mind?' she asked as casually as she could.

'I thought I might cook for you.'

'You, cook?' she said, somehow surprised.

'I'm a good cook,' he said a little stiffly, and she relented and smiled.

'I'm sure you are. That sounds lovely. What time?'

'Whenever. Six? Seven?'

'Make it seven. I'll look forward to it. Oh, and I don't like kidney beans.'

'Good. Something else we've got in common,' he said, and with a farewell wink that made her knees go weak, he headed for the lift and left her to it.

Molly didn't know what to wear. Casual, of course, because he was cooking for her at his house and that didn't call for anything dressy, but on the other hand she didn't want to be too casual and offend him.

Whatever, nothing fitted, nothing looked good, nothing seemed to suit her.

She ended up with almost the entire contents of her wardrobe on her bed and a huge crisis of confidence, and in the midst of it the phone rang.

'Hello?' she said, and was greeted with Angie's voice bubbling with curiosity.

'Hi, sweets. How are you?'

'I'm fine.'

'How's the plan going?' she asked, cutting straight to the chase as ever, and Molly laughed.

'I'm not sure. I'm having dinner with him in half an hour—he's cooking for me, and I've got my entire wardrobe on my bed and I just look awful in everything. I'm going to end up going in my uniform at this rate.'

'Rubbish. Have you got that blue thing?'

'The jersey dress?'

'Yes—the straight one with the floppy neck that makes you look like a stick insect with boobs. Wear that.'

'Really?' Molly said, staring at it doubtfully. 'It's a bit—'

'Sexy is what it is,' Angie told her bluntly. 'Wear it—and ring me after the weekend and tell me what's happened.'

'You're just nosy.'

'No, I just care. I love you. Have fun.'

The line went dead, and Molly cradled the phone, smiling wryly. Have fun.

OK. In the blue dress.

Oh, yipes.

She put it on, eyeing herself critically in the mirror and sucking in her stomach. Hmm. There was nothing she could do about it, she'd had three children—and one of them was his. That was one of the key things about stress management—change the things you could, and learn to live with the things you couldn't. Her stomach she'd learned to live with.

She turned round and peered over her shoulder, and decided the back view was OK, and it did make her bust look good. 'All right, I'll wear it,' she said to the absent Angie. Slipping on her shoes, she went downstairs, shrugged into her jacket and let herself out.

She'd picked up a bottle of wine at the supermarket last night, but no doubt it was the wrong colour for what Sam was planning. Never mind, it was the thought that counted and she couldn't really take him flowers.

And then she started wondering what, exactly, he was planning for that evening, and her heart went into overdrive.

*   *   *

Sam was wondering if he'd gone crazy. He'd bought steak and salad and baby new potatoes, nothing complicated, and a frozen chocolate dessert that couldn't possibly go wrong, and yet he was nervous.

It took him a moment to work out that it had nothing to do with the food. Food like that he could cook with his eyes shut.

No, it was Molly—or, more precisely, Molly's proposition.

It was the Bakers' fault, of course. All that happy families stuff this time last week had got to him, and after a week of reasoning he'd distilled it down to one significant fact.

He was alone, and he hated it. Some people thrived on it, but he didn't. He needed company, needed companionship, needed—hell, yes, he needed sex. There was nothing wrong with that, and Molly was offering, for heaven's sake! Only a saint would turn her down.

So here he was, trying to cook her a meal tonight with his mind quite definitely on other things! If it wasn't a charred disaster, it deserved to be.

He uncorked the wine, sniffed it and left it to breathe near the Aga. The potatoes were boiled and keeping warm in the bottom oven, smothered in butter and olive oil, the salad was in the bowl ready to dress, the steaks were in the fridge where the cat wouldn't get them, and all he needed now was Molly.

Right on cue, the doorbell rang and he went to let her in.

It was still daylight, sort of, and the last rays of the sun were gilding her skin and touching her hair with fire. She smiled and held up a bottle of wine, and as he took it his hand touched hers and heat shot through him.

'Thanks. Come in,' he said gruffly, and stepped back so

she could pass him. The light fragrance of her skin lingered in the air, and he felt his gut contract. 'I'm pottering in the kitchen,' he told her. 'Go on through.'

He followed her, unable to take his eyes off her ankles under the hem of that dress. Was it a dress? He thought so, and then she slipped the jacket off and he got a closer look at it, and heat slammed into him all over again.

He put the bottle down with a little thunk and took her jacket, hanging it over the back of a chair to give himself time to get his composure back. Then he turned to her and dredged up a smile.

'You look lovely tonight,' he said, and soft colour brushed her cheeks.

'It's ancient.'

'I wasn't looking at the dress,' he said, and her colour rose again, her eyes widening and darkening, her lips parting softly.

'Are you flirting with me?' she said after a moment, and he gave a wry grin.

'No. I was just talking without thinking. I do that sometimes. My mouth moves without bothering to engage my brain.'

'I'm not complaining,' she said, and he realised she was smiling.

He felt the tension going out of his body. Good grief. At this rate, he might almost enjoy the evening. He poured her a glass of wine—just a small one, she said, because she was driving later, but not if the gods were on his side—and put the cast-iron skillet on the hob to heat.

'How do you like your steak?' he asked her over his shoulder, and she turned away from Jack's latest offering on the front of the fridge and came over to him, threatening his sanity with that delicate fragrance and the nearness of her body.

'Slightly rare,' she murmured, peering at the pan. 'What's the Aga like to cook with?'

He gave a slightly strained laugh. He was dying here, and she wanted to talk about the Aga? 'I'm still getting used to it,' he confessed, and held the first steak suspended over the skillet. 'I should mind yourself, this might splatter a bit.'

She stepped back, giving his sanity a little elbow-room, and he dropped the meat into the hot pan and pulled the plates and the potatoes out of the bottom oven.

'You could dress the salad,' he said over his shoulder, and watched out of the corner of his eye as she drizzled olive oil and balsamic vinegar over the leaves, crunched pepper and salt over the top then tossed it all together.

She was a joy to watch, he thought, staring at her, and then remembered the steaks in the nick of time.

'That was gorgeous,' she said, sitting back and smiling at him over the top of their empty plates.

'Good. More wine?'

Molly shook her head. 'No. I'm driving, remember? I could kill a coffee, though.'

Sam laughed and stood up, putting on the kettle and rinsing out the cafetière with hot water. Moments later it was ready, and he picked up the tray, complete with after-dinner mints, and headed for the door.

'Come on, we'll go in the study, since you seem to like it so much.'

She followed him through and made herself comfortable on the sofa, sitting with her feet curled under her bottom and looking totally relaxed. No. Not totally. There was an inner tension there, he noticed, and he felt his own tension rise a notch in response.

He handed her her coffee and sat down at the other end

of the sofa, the chocolates on the cushion between them, and for a moment neither of them said anything.

Then, without engaging his brain again, his mouth said, 'That affair you were talking about—is the offer still open?'

She went utterly still, and then, setting her coffee down with great deliberation, she looked across at him. 'Why?'

He put his own coffee down, safely out of the way, and met the warm caramel caress of her eyes. 'Because, if it is, I'd like to take you up on it.'

She stared at him unblinkingly for a moment, then she swallowed, revealing that tension again. 'OK—but before we do, there's something you ought to know.'

He nodded slowly, his heart racing out of control. Stay calm, he thought. 'OK. Tell me.'

She took a deep, steadying breath and closed her eyes, then opened them again, staring down at her fingers. They were knotted together, he noticed, and he wondered what on earth she had to say.

'I'm thirty-three,' she announced eventually.

He blinked and stared at her. 'I'd already worked that one out, being reasonably good at maths,' he teased gently.

'And I've had three children.'

Oh, lord, the silly woman was worried that he wouldn't find her attractive! 'I know. I was responsible for the last one—remember?'

'And I'm a widow.'

He didn't come back quite so quick on that one, because suddenly the conversation was taking a different tack and he wasn't sure any longer where it was headed. 'I know,' he said finally, his voice gentle. 'Is that a problem?'

She looked up at him then, her eyes wide and wary. 'I don't know. You see, it's a bit silly. I'm thirty-three, the mother of three children, and a widow—and I've never done this before. I don't know what to do.'

So that was it. He gave a little huff of laughter in relief. 'Is that all? I'm sure the principle hasn't changed that much in ten years. It's like riding a bike—you don't forget how.'

She shook her head. 'No. You don't understand. I mean, I've *never* done it before, Sam. I don't know how. I'm a virgin.'

He felt his jaw sag, and snapped it shut. A virgin? But...

'You were married—you had Libby.'

'By IVF. You do know Mick was a paraplegic, surely?'

'Yes, but—not when you met him? There's a picture of you on your mantelpiece, standing with your arms round each other.'

'That was before the accident. Before we fell in love and got married. Libby was conceived by ICSI—intra-cytoplasmic sperm injection—using sperm harvested from Mick by syringe. Mick never made love to me, Sam, he couldn't—and there's been no one else.'

Sam felt strangled. He went to loosen his tie and realised he wasn't wearing one. He looked at her again, and the full impact of what she'd just said hit him like a sledge-hammer.

'Why me?' he asked, his voice rough with shock.

She shrugged. 'Why not? You're a good friend, a reasonably attractive specimen...'

He nearly choked. 'Well, thanks for that,' he muttered, and she laughed softly.

'My pleasure. I'm pretty sure I'm not going to get any nasty diseases from you—and anyway, I've had your child,' she added softly, 'so why not you? You're the obvious choice.'

He dragged his eyes away from her and picked up his

coffee, giving it very much more attention than it deserved. Or maybe not. Perhaps it was just what he needed—a bit of caffeine to clear his head after all that wine.

It was nothing to do with the wine, of course. He'd only had one glass, and he felt stone cold sober. Still, he drank the coffee for something safe to do and, reaching for the jug, he topped up his mug.

'More?'

'I haven't drunk this yet,' she pointed out.

'No. Well—um—chocolate?'

'Sam, talk to me.'

He shook his head to clear it. 'Molly, I can't. I need to think.'

'Why? Don't tell me you're going to change your mind!'

'Maybe.' He looked at her solemnly. 'Molly, this changes things, you must see that.'

'Why? I'm an adult, Sam, and so are you. We're both free. It doesn't change anything—unless the idea of making love to a virgin turns you off.'

'Turns me off?' he exclaimed, jackknifing up and pacing to the window. 'Hell, Molly, don't be silly.'

'So what's the problem, then?'

He shrugged. 'It should be something special.'

'So make it special,' she said softly. 'Please, Sam. I've waited such a long time. I'm thirty-three—don't you think it's about time?'

He turned, and she was behind him, so close he nearly fell over her. For a moment he stood there, then with a ragged groan he drew her into his arms, tucked her head under his chin and hugged her, hideously aware of her warmth and softness, the firm press of her breasts against his chest, the gentle swell of her hips...

'OK,' he sighed, too weak to turn her down, 'but not

now. Not like this—please. Your first time should be special.'

'It will be.'

'Yes—but not tonight. Tomorrow. Give me time to prepare things.'

'You'll change your mind.'

'No. No, I won't, I promise. Not a chance. I just have to do it right this time, Molly.'

'This time?' she asked, and he sighed. He might as well tell her.

'When I lost my virginity, I was seventeen, and so was the girl. It was the first time for both of us, and it was messy and uncomfortable and undignified. I didn't even know her name, and I never saw her again, so I never had a chance to apologise. I vowed then that if I ever made love to another virgin, I'd do it properly—and I will. That's a promise. Now go home, there's a good girl, before I lose my resolve. I'll ring you. Go.'

He fetched her jacket, helped her into it and turned her into his arms, lowering his mouth to hers for a teasing, tempting kiss that left them both aching for more.

'Go on,' he whispered, and pushed her gently out of the door. He saw her to her car, closing the driver's door with some regret, and then, as her taillights disappeared through the gate, he closed his eyes and sighed.

His hands were shaking—his whole body was shaking—and he nearly got into his car and followed her. He must have been mad to send her away.

Still, it would be worth it—if he survived the suspense!

Molly went to work the next morning in a daze. She'd spent the night torn between anticipation and the fear of disappointing Sam, and when her alarm went off she was only too relieved. She arrived at work to find the place crawling with newspaper reporters and film crews from the local television stations, and went into the sanctuary of the ward to find out what was going on.

'So who's the celebrity in labour?' she asked, but Sue shook her head.

'No celebrity. A baby girl was found last night left in the loo at a twenty-four-hour supermarket. She was very new—minutes rather than hours old, and the cord was hacked through and not even tied, so she was very lucky to survive. They think she'd been born there, but nobody had noticed anything strange.'

'Really? Must have been a multigravida,' Molly said thoughtfully. 'A first-time mum would have made too much fuss, surely, and been in there too long.'

'Maybe. The worrying thing is, there was no sign of the placenta. She might have flushed it down the loo, but they're a bit big to go willingly.'

'Oh, lord. Oh, poor thing—whatever must she be going through? Where's the baby? Special Care?'

Sue shook her head. 'No—in here. SCBU's full, and she seems to be full term. We've given her milk from the breast-milk bank. Josh Lancaster's been in and checked her over, and he's happy that she hasn't suffered any adverse affects, but she should be with her mum.'

'And her mum,' Molly said, troubled, 'should be in here, being checked over. What if she had a retained placenta? It doesn't bear thinking about. Oh, well.' She shrugged the thought aside. 'So what else is going on? Any labours I should know about?'

'No, it's really quiet. You could cuddle the baby and feed her, if you elbow everyone else out of the way.'

Molly laughed. 'I might just do that. I always seem to be too busy to cuddle the babies.'

She went into the nursery and found the little scrap on

her own. All the other babies were with their mothers, and there were precious few of them anyway. She'd never known it so quiet, she thought, and wished it would hot up a bit, to take her mind off Sam and tonight.

Not until she'd had a cuddle with the baby, though!

She was starting to stir, her little arms flailing from time to time, her mouth working rhythmically. Molly glanced at the notes, saw she was due for a feed and was on her way to get it when a nursery nurse came in with a bottle.

'May I?' Molly asked with a smile, and the girl handed the bottle over reluctantly and left her to it. She scooped the little thing out of her clear Perspex crib and settled into the nursing chair, cuddling the baby against her as she brushed the teat against her mouth. Her rosebud lips fastened hungrily on the teat and she sucked, then coughed.

'Too fast for you, sweetheart? Slow down a little, don't be so impatient.'

The crooning seemed to soothe her, and she settled back to suckle quietly while Molly stared down at her and wondered how anyone could walk away from her child and leave it in a public toilet. What on earth was she going through?

'Molly?'

Her heart skidded to a halt and picked up again, thrashing against her ribs. She looked up as Sam came towards her, hunkering down beside her and stroking the baby's cheek with the back of his finger. The tender gesture nearly undid her. 'Is this our mystery baby?' he asked softly.

Molly nodded. 'Yes—poor little thing. I'm just giving her a feed. What are you doing here? I didn't realise you were in.'

'Oh, I'm on call. I've come in to check a patient with an elevated temperature post-op—probably peritonitis. It was a nasty, messy operation that had been left too late, so it doesn't surprise me, even with the blockbuster antibiotics she's on. I'm on my way home now, but I wanted to talk to you about tonight.'

Oh, lord, he's changed his mind, she thought, and disappointment washed over her in a wave. Then she met his eyes, and realised she was mistaken.

'I'll pick you up at seven,' he said, his voice rough and low. 'Wear something suitable for dinner and dancing.'

'Dancing?'

'Don't you dance?'

'I didn't realise we were going out.'

He smiled, his eyes smouldering. 'We aren't. I'll see you later.'

Her heart thumped against her ribs, and she watched him go in a stunned silence. Dinner and dancing? At home? Wow. It was just beginning to dawn on her what he'd meant by 'doing it right', and she wondered what else was in store for her.

She burped and changed the baby on autopilot, and put her down to sleep again after a little cuddle to settle her. There was nothing to do on the ward, so she went into the empty delivery room and sorted through the equipment and tried not to guess what Sam was planning.

She blew up the gym balls that were used to support women in labour if they wanted to hang over something, and checked that all the necessary delivery packs were there and nothing was missing—and thought about Sam.

She was just coming out onto the ward again when someone came through the doors at the other end of the corridor and stood there, looking round a little wildly.

Even from here Molly could see that she was distressed, and instinctively she realised that this was the mother of the abandoned baby. She was looking for the nursery, Molly guessed, and there was no way she was going to

snatch her baby back and leave without medical attention
if Molly had anything to do with it.

'That girl's here. Tell Security to watch out for her, and
get Sam—now. He might still be in the building,' she said
out of the corner of her mouth as she walked past the ward
clerk, and without hesitating she went up to the girl and
gave her a casual smile.

'Hi. Have you come to visit someone?' she said, giving
her a reason to be there, and the girl nodded, her eyes
sliding away from Molly's.

'Well, why don't you come and have a cup of tea while
you wait? It isn't visiting for a few more minutes, and I
was just having one.' She led the girl into the kitchen,
pushed the door shut and turned on the kettle, propping
herself in the way so she couldn't escape. The girl was
chalk-white and twitchy, and Molly was worried about her.
How to proceed, though?

'It's been a bit of a dramatic night,' she said casually,
wondering how hard she could push it. 'We've had a baby
brought in without her mother. Lovely little thing—I've
just fed her. She's really pretty—a bit like you.'

The girl went still. 'So—she's all right?'

'Yes, she's fine—but we're worried about the mother.
She probably needs help, and we can't help her unless
she'll let us.'

The girl met her eyes then, defeat written in them, and
tears spilt over and ran down her cheeks. 'I can't keep
her.'

Molly's heart went out to the girl. 'Maybe not,' she said
softly, 'but someone ought to look after you in the meantime. Can I have a look at you? I'm a midwife—I deliver
babies and look after the mums.'

'I can't be a mum. I'm only seventeen—my parents
think I've been at art college, but I left. I told them I'd

gone round Europe for the summer—part of my course. They'd kill me.'

'I doubt it. I've got a daughter, and I wouldn't kill her.'

She shook her head. 'Dad's a minister. Mum's a teacher. They'll be so ashamed of me.'

She put her hand over her mouth to hold in the sobs, and the other crept to her still-distended abdomen. 'I feel really ill—I want my mum…'

'Come on, sweetheart, let's sort you out,' Molly said, and, putting her arm round her shoulders, she led the girl across the corridor into one of the little side rooms. As she went in, she caught sight of Sam hurrying towards her, and she shook her head slightly.

He slowed, and she knew he'd hover in earshot, so she left the door open a crack.

'Right, my love, hop up on the bed and let's have a look at you.'

She didn't get any further. With a tiny cry the girl crumpled, and to Molly's horror the floor beneath her turned dark crimson.

'Sam!' she yelled, but he was already there, lifting the girl onto the bed, elevating her legs and pressing firmly into her abdomen to try and halt the haemorrhage.

'I'll have to take her up to Theatre—come with me, we don't have time to wait for the ODA.'

The next few minutes were tense, and Molly worked alongside the theatre team to get lines in and fluids into the girl to support her system until blood supplies arrived. Finally Sam was satisfied that the haemorrhaging had stopped and he'd removed the placental fragment that had been causing it, and her uterus was contracting down well.

'OK, thanks, everyone,' he said. Stripping off his gloves and mask, he threw Molly a grin. 'Thanks for that. She should be down with you in about half an hour. Any idea of the story?'

Molly shrugged. 'She wants her mother, that's all I know.'

'Did you get a number?'

'Nothing. There wasn't time. She is going to make it, Sam, isn't she?'

'Of course she is. I'll get her down to you straight away, and you can reunite her with her baby—if she wants that.'

'I don't know if she does, but she ought to,' Molly said. 'She may not know she wants it yet, but she will, later in life, and it could be too late then. She needs to talk to her mother first before she makes a decision either way.'

Molly went back to the ward, prepared all the paperwork for the girl's admission and went to see the sleeping baby. 'Your mum's here, little one,' she said softly. 'I hope she can love you enough to find a way to stay with you.'

There would be hundreds of couples out there—probably thousands—who would have her if not, Molly knew, but somehow she felt that that poor girl needed her baby, whatever her parents might feel. Surely a minister and a teacher would have enough human-kindness and understanding to support their daughter through this?

Molly could only hope so, for all their sakes.

The girl was called Rosalind, and her parents came instantly when they were phoned. Molly was there, helping her to feed her baby, when the door opened and they came in, and a more tearful and loving reunion it was hard to imagine.

'Silly, silly girl,' her father kept saying, tears streaming down his cheeks, and her mother just held her and the baby and rocked them and sobbed.

'A granddaughter—I can't believe it,' she said, and sobbed again.

'I'll get you some tea,' Molly said, and left them alone together for a few minutes. When she went back in Rosalind was explaining the circumstances of the baby's conception, and it seemed she'd been the victim of a date-rape drug.

'I have no idea who the father is,' she was saying. 'There wasn't anyone in particular, just a whole group of lads at this party, and I don't remember anything about it. I just woke up feeling—really dirty...'

She started to cry again, and Molly took the baby gently from her and tucked her up in her crib by the bed. There would be plenty of time to cuddle her later. Just now, the poor girl needed to talk, and her parents needed to listen.

'Ring the bell if you need anything,' she said, and went out, almost bumping into Sam in the doorway.

'I gather her parents are here,' he murmured.

'Yes. Can you leave them for a few minutes?'

'If I can persuade a pretty young midwife to make me a cup of coffee in the meantime.'

'Sorry, you're out of luck, I'm the only one free,' she said, and he chuckled and followed her into the kitchen, kicking the door shut and turning her into his arms.

'That's a glass door,' she pointed out, but it was only a small glass panel, and he leant against it, obscuring them from view while he kissed her thoroughly and systematically.

'That's just to keep you ticking over till tonight,' he said, and then, without waiting for coffee, he opened the door, backed out into the corridor grinning wickedly and left her there, her body clamouring for more...

CHAPTER NINE

SAM'S car pulled up on her drive at two minutes past seven, and as Molly watched him walk up to the door, her first reaction was relief.

He was wearing a dinner suit. Wear something suitable for dancing, he'd said, and absolutely the only thing in her wardrobe that qualified even slightly was a ballgown she'd bought in a charity shop for a Stoke Mandeville fundraiser two years ago.

So that's what she was wearing, a sleek, slightly A-line skirt with a fishtail pleat in the back, and a boned, fitted basque that fitted her like a glove and did incredible things for her figure. She'd been hovering in her bedroom, waiting to see if she was hopelessly overdressed.

Her immediate problem dealt with, she allowed herself to study him as he strode purposefully towards her door, and her mouth went dry.

What was it about men in dinner suits? No, not men. Sam. He looked stunning. The stark contrast of the white shirt against his skin, the cut of the suit emphasising the breadth of his shoulders and hinting at the lean, powerful muscles of his legs—he looked magnificent, she thought, and she felt suddenly totally out of her depth.

Like a lamb to the slaughter, she picked up her bag, checked her reflection one last time and headed for the stairs, her long coat covering the dress and giving her something to hide behind. Dredging up a smile, she opened the door.

'Hi—you're ready,' he said, sounding surprised, and she smiled faintly.

'Of course I'm ready,' she said, wishing it were true, and stepped outside. The night air was cool, and she shivered with anticipation. He turned up her coat collar, snuggling it closer, and brushed a teasing kiss over her lips.

'Your taxi awaits, ma'am,' he murmured, and, closing the door behind them, he ushered her to the car and settled her in it.

He's treating me like royalty, she thought, and stifled the sudden desperate urge to giggle. He opened the other door and slid in behind the wheel, throwing her a fleeting smile before pulling away. They hardly spoke on the journey to his house, and she got the strangest feeling that he was as nervous as she was.

Sam? Nervous?

They pulled up outside his house, and he ushered her inside and through to the kitchen.

'Sorry it's not very glamorous,' he said with an apologetic grin, 'but I have a choice of leaving you in the sitting room alone, or having you with me in the kitchen, and I've just got a few finishing touches to put to things. Let me take your coat.'

Molly felt her chin come up a notch. Would he approve, or would he think she'd gone totally over the top?

She turned her back to him and allowed him to slide it from her shoulders, and his soft intake of breath gave her confidence. She turned back to him and was gratified to see the warmth of appreciation in his eyes.

'You look beautiful,' he said, his voice gruff, and he draped her coat over the back of a chair and eased a finger round his collar under the bow-tie as if it was strangling him. 'Let me get you a drink.'

He pulled a bottle out of an ice bucket in the sink, and deftly twisted off the wire cage holding the cork.

'Bubbly?'

'Mmm—with a difference,' he said, twisting off the cork inside a teatowel and pouring the smoking liquid into two tall flutes, handing her one. As the bubbles settled, she could see a thin, brown stick bobbing in the glass. She sniffed curiously.

'Vanilla?' she said, and he smiled.

'It's an aphrodisiac,' he murmured, and lifted his glass to hers. 'Here's to tonight—may it be a night to remember.'

She met his smouldering eyes over the top of the glass and wondered why she didn't just catch fire. Her nerves evaporated, driven off by the intensity of his eyes, and she smiled back a little unsteadily. They didn't need an aphrodisiac.

'To tonight,' she concurred, and, without taking her eyes from his, she sipped the wine.

It tasted—interesting. Different. Fragrant and heady— and if she wasn't careful, that's exactly where it would end up, going to her head. She lowered the glass.

'So, what else is on the menu?' she asked, even more curious now.

He smiled and tapped the side of his nose. 'You'll see.'

'I will—I intend to watch you.'

'No. You'll put me off. You look too damn beautiful in that dress, you're distracting me to bits. Go and sit on the other side of the table before I forget all my good intentions and make love to you on it.'

A warm tide of colour ran over her skin, and she retreated to the safety of the far side of what until then had been just a simple piece of furniture. She regarded it warily, then with curiosity.

'No,' he said, his voice gruff, and turned back to the stove, leaving her with a temptress's smile playing around her lips.

She tested the air. Asparagus, and something vaguely seafoody—not fish, but something that teased at her memory. Scallops? He'd just put a tray into the top oven, and he was steaming something on the hob—the asparagus, she'd bet.

He put a little pan on beside the asparagus, then poured the contents into a bowl, lifted out the bright, fresh spears and placed them into a warmed dish and turned to her, clicking his heels and smiling.

'Dinner is served, madam,' he announced.

'Shall I lay the table?' she asked, and he chuckled softly.

'It's done. Bring the champagne.'

She followed him, the two flutes and the bottle in hand, and he led her into a room she'd never seen previously. It was dark, and as her eyes adjusted she heard the flick of a lighter and the soft glow of the candles illuminated the table, casting an intimate pool of light that sparkled on crystal and silver.

Good heavens. Sam really had pulled out all the stops. There were crisply folded linen napkins on the tablemats, and fingerbowls that he filled with hot water from a flask. The scent of citrus filled the air, and he seated her and then took his place at right angles to her, close enough that their knees brushed as he sat down.

He placed the dish of asparagus between them, picked up a spear and dipped it in the butter, then held it to her lips.

Oh, good grief. He was going to feed her...

She opened her mouth and bit into the sweet, juicy stem, butter running onto her lips. He brushed it away with a blunt fingertip, then touched it to his tongue. Heat shot through her. How could eating be so incredibly erotic? she wondered, but this was just the appetiser.

She picked up a spear and fed it to him, absurdly aroused by the sight of his strong, white teeth biting cleanly through the pale green flesh. My goodness, she thought, at this rate we won't get through the first course.

She'd reckoned without Sam. He fed her the last morsel, left her with a murmured command to stay put, and came back moments later with a steaming dish of scallop shells, topped with crisp, golden breadcrumbs and smelling absolutely heavenly.

'Scallops and oysters,' he told her, 'with wild rocket and basil salad.'

'Aphrodisiacs?' she asked, knowing the answer before he smiled acknowledgement.

'I found a very interesting website. Open wide.'

The flavour burst on her tongue, and she picked up her fork and returned the favour. 'Whatever did we do before the internet?' she asked, and he chuckled.

'I don't know. Open.'

Aphrodisiac or not, she thought she'd never tasted anything so delicious in her life. He was right, he was a good cook—and his presentation was faultless.

The dishes were cleared away, and he reappeared with a plate of fresh fruit—strawberries, frosted grapes, slices of pear, apple and banana, juicy triangles of pineapple— and in the centre of the plate was a dish of melted dessert chocolate.

Sam poured her a glass of a dark red wine and she raised her eyebrows.

'Cabernet sauvignon—it's a very good one, very fruity, lots of body. It's stunning with the chocolate.'

She laughed. 'I believe you,' she said. 'You've been right about everything else.'

He dipped a slice of pear into the chocolate and held it to her lips, and the contrast of the bitter chocolate with the sweet, crisp flesh of the pear was astonishing. She sipped the wine, nodded and set it down.

'You're right. Here.'

Molly fed him a strawberry, then some of the pineapple, and as he bit into it a dribble of chocolate ran down his chin.

'You're a messy eater,' she said gently, and, leaning forwards, she stroked it away with her tongue.

A deep groan erupted from his chest and he leant towards her, but she backed away, shaking her head. 'Uh-uh. We haven't finished yet.'

'How do you know that?'

'I'm sure you've got some trick up your sleeve with the coffee,' she said, and he gave a strained laugh.

'How did you guess? Are you ready for it?'

She chuckled. 'The coffee?'

'The coffee.'

'Absolutely.'

He whisked away her chair for her with all the skill of a *maître d'*, and she allowed him to lead her to the sitting room.

Soft music was playing, and on the coffee-table there was an array of petits fours, tiny truffles and marzipan fruits dipped in dark chocolate—not the chemical-flavoured bought variety, she realised, but home-made, sculpted by his own highly skilled and industrious hand.

'When on earth did you find time?' she asked as he came back into the room with a tray and set it down beside the sweets.

'Nothing took long,' he told her, and she realised it was probably true. Everything had been very simple, apart from the scallops and oysters, and even that was probably a quick dish to prepare.

It was the thought that had gone into it which touched her, the care and attention to detail. Her eyes filled with tears and she blinked them away.

'Coffee,' he said, passing her a tiny little cup filled with a black, fragrant brew with a touch of...

'Nutmeg?' she said, puzzled, and then shook her head when he smiled. 'Don't tell me—the website. It's got a lot to answer for.'

He picked up a little marzipan orange and held it to her lips, but he didn't release it. Instead he waited until she bit into it, then put the other half in his mouth.

She swallowed, the sweet almond paste gliding down her throat, fragrant and smooth. She sipped her coffee, hot and strong and strangely refreshing, and then, picking up a truffle, she held it to his lips and copied his actions.

It left her fingers covered in chocolate, and he caught her hand and drew it to his lips, their eyes locked, suckling each fingertip in turn until her body hummed like a bow-string. Heat pooled in her and a tiny moan escaped her lips.

Without releasing her hand, he drew her to her feet and into his arms, his hands resting lightly against her spine. They swayed gently to the music, their bodies scarcely touching, the warmth of his hands, the hard brush of his thighs against hers and the feel of his shoulders under her hands their only points of contact.

Easing back, she reached up and caught one end of his bow-tie and pulled it slowly undone, then slipped the button free and pressed a light, taunting kiss against the hollow of his throat.

His hands slid lower, easing her against him, and she

felt the heat of his arousal burning through the fabric of her dress.

His head dipped, his breath warm against her ear, and she felt the soft graze of his jaw against her throat. He nuzzled closer, his lips burning a trail down over her collar-bone and back up, past her ear, over her cheekbone, her eyes, her chin, then finally settling against her mouth with a ragged sigh.

He tasted of dark, bitter chocolate, fragrant coffee and sweet-scented almonds, and the combination was unbelievably erotic.

His tongue traced her lips, coaxing them apart, and then he deepened the kiss, the moist, hot velvet of his tongue delving into her mouth again and again, challenging her, duelling with her, until she grew bolder and returned the caress.

His groan erupted against her lips, his hands urgent now, trembling against her as they cupped her breasts, and she threaded her fingers through the soft, silken strands of his hair and drew him closer, clinging to him in case she should fall.

He lifted his head, resisting her, and stared down into her face with eyes of fire.

'Molly, I need you,' he said, and the simplicity of the words nearly brought her to her knees.

'I need you, too, Sam—now, please…'

He released her, easing away from her with obvious reluctance. Holding out his hand, he led her through the house without a word, up the stairs, along the landing and into his room.

'Close your eyes,' he murmured, and she heard the scrape of his lighter wheel against the flint. 'You can open them now,' he said, and she did so, knowing what she'd find and yet still touched by the beauty of the flickering flames in every corner of the room.

Big church candles, tiny floating lights drifting in bowls of water, tall, slender tapers in simple glass holders—each was beautiful, but the total effect was incredible, unbelievably romantic—and in the midst of them all was the bed.

It was huge, a beautiful mahogany four-poster just made for loving, and the simple ivory bedspread was scattered with rose petals.

'Oh, Sam,' she whispered, and looked up into those amazing blue eyes that seemed to reflect the flame of every single candle, focusing them all into a fire so bright she thought it would consume her.

'Undress for me,' she whispered, and he gave a gruff, startled laugh.

'I thought that was my line,' he said, but his hands came up and stripped away the bow-tie she'd already undone, his fingers trembling too much to manage the buttons.

'Help me,' he pleaded, and she stepped closer, slipping the buttons free one by one until his chest was revealed to her. She slid her hands inside the fabric, parting it, and pressed her lips to the warm, smooth skin. There was a light scatter of hair in the centre, just enough to tease her lips, and she moved the shirt aside until she found one taut, flat male nipple and took it gently in her teeth.

He groaned and rocked against her, and suddenly her patience was gone. She needed him, and she needed him now. She was done with subtlety and foreplay, and she thought if she didn't feel him against her skin in the next few seconds, she'd surely die. She dragged the shirt aside, whimpering when it caught on his wrists, and he wrenched it free.

His trousers followed, kicked aside with his shoes and socks, leaving him utterly naked and breath-stealingly beautiful.

'How does this come off?' he asked, his chest rising and falling sharply as he stared in frustration at her basque.

'There's a zip—at the back.'

He found it, sliding it down until it parted, and the top fell away, spilling her breasts into his waiting hands.

'Dear God, Molly,' he breathed, and then his lips found them, his breath hot against her skin, then cold as it fanned across the damp trail of his tongue. His fingers found the zip on her skirt and it fell to a pool at her feet, leaving her standing there dressed only in a tiny black lace thong that Angie had sent her for Christmas as a joke.

It didn't seem like a joke now. His eyes flared, and he drew her into his arms and held her there for a moment, his body almost vibrating with the tension running through it.

'Lie on the bed,' he ordered softly, and she climbed up and lay down, suddenly self-conscious in front of him. Molly knew her figure wasn't bad, but three pregnancies had left inevitable consequences.

'You're beautiful,' he said, his voice raw with need. He closed his eyes, as if he was counting to ten, she thought, and then he opened them again and reached out to the bedside table, lifting a foil packet in trembling fingers.

'No,' she said, reaching out and covering his hands with hers. 'You don't need that. I went on the Pill two weeks ago—just in case. I didn't want anything between us.'

His breath left his body in a harsh gust. Dropping the

little wrapper, he knelt at her feet and drew the tiny scrap of lace slowly down her legs. It went the way of their other clothes, and then he came down beside her and drew her into his arms, the heat of the contact making them both gasp.

His mouth found hers, fierce with hunger, and then he lifted his head and stared down into her eyes. 'God help me, Molly, I'm not going to last ten seconds.'

'Neither am I. I want you, Sam—please. Now.'

He moved over her, his hands threading through her hair, fanning it on the pillow, and his eyes locked with hers. Then he was there, inside her, with her every inch of that long, glorious climb to oblivion, and when she reached the top he was there with her still, his harsh cry mingling with her own as she crested the peak and fell headlong in his arms.

Sam was stunned. He'd never known anything like it in his life, and he didn't think it was anything to do with all the preparation or scene-setting. He had a feeling that if he'd just taken her there and then on the kitchen table when she'd arrived, it would have been the same.

He'd have to try it later, he thought, his free hand idly stroking the smooth, satin skin of her back. The other hand was meshed with hers, cradled on his chest, and one slim, silky leg was wedged firmly between his thighs.

Molly was asleep, and he was taking advantage of it to get his emotions in order. He snorted softly. Not a chance. There was no way his emotions would ever be the same again, he realised, and the thought terrified him.

He loved her.

It was that simple, and that complicated. So much for

their no-strings, someone-to-do-things-with affair. His fingers tightened on hers, and she lifted her head and looked deep into his eyes, as if she was searching for something.

'What's wrong?' she murmured.

'Nothing.' He drew her closer. 'Come here.'

He made love to her again, slowly this time, kissing every inch of her until she wept with frustration, then taking her to the peak again and again until he couldn't stand it any more and went with her, tumbling even further into the fathomless abyss of love.

'Can I ask you something incredibly intrusive and personal?'

Molly stopped drawing circles on Sam's chest and looked up at him in the grey morning light. He looked troubled, and she pressed her lips to his rough, stubbled jaw. 'Of course.'

'It's about your marriage. Tell me to go to hell if you like, but last night, whenever I touched you, whatever I did, it was as if it was the first time—for *everything*. I mean, I know he was paraplegic, but so many of the things I did with you, he could have done, and yet you felt so incredibly—I don't know. Untouched?'

'Because I was,' she said honestly. 'We didn't do anything.'

'Never? Why?' Sam asked, sounding astounded. 'If that had been me, I'm sure I would have wanted to touch you, to give you pleasure. It would have been its own reward for me.'

For a moment she didn't reply. She couldn't, because she was dragged back into the past, back to Mick and that awful, heart-rending night.

'Maybe,' she said eventually. 'Or maybe not. He tried once. He said it wasn't fair to me, that I shouldn't be denied a sex life just because he couldn't do anything, and he kissed me and...' She broke off, the words somehow too hard to find. 'We gave up in the end. It just felt all wrong, when I could give nothing back. It didn't seem important enough, and so we just went to sleep.'

She fell silent, hoping Sam would leave it at that, but he didn't, of course.

'There's more, isn't there?' he murmured.

She nodded slowly, reluctantly. 'I woke up later because he'd got out of bed. He did that sometimes, because he didn't sleep well, and he usually pottered about and made a drink, read a book, something like that, and then he'd come back to bed later. I suppose I must have dozed off again, and then a noise woke me—a terrible noise, like a wounded animal.'

Sam's arm tightened around her, his hand splaying out on her back, comforting her, as if he knew what was coming.

'I found him in the kitchen, on the floor in the corner. At first I thought he'd fallen, but he'd dragged himself there as if he was trying to hide from the pain. I thought something terrible had happened to him—which I suppose it had. He told me to go away, to leave him. I wouldn't, I covered him with a blanket and curled up with him to keep him warm, because he was freezing and he couldn't feel it.'

'Couldn't you get him back to bed?'

She shook her head. 'No. He wouldn't move, and he was far too heavy to lift, so I stayed with him. He wouldn't talk to me, he just kept shuddering, and in the end I got angry and yelled at him. I was worried sick, and he wouldn't share it with me, and I couldn't take any more. He told me to leave—said it was over. I knew he didn't mean it, so I made him talk to me. I nagged and bullied until he broke down and let it all out, how he wasn't man enough for me, how I deserved better, a real man, someone who could give me children—rubbish like that. So I told him how much I loved him, and I asked him to marry me.'

'You weren't married?'

Molly shook her head again. 'Not then. It took me a week or so to wear him down, but finally he agreed, after we'd found out that we could have a child by IVF. We could easily afford it, because of the compensation payout after his accident, and it took away his strongest argument.'

'So you got married.'

'Yes. A few weeks later, but he never touched me again, apart from the occasional affectionate kiss. It was like some unwritten agreement, and we both respected it. Two years after that we had Libby, and it changed him completely. He felt like a man again, he said, and he was a wonderful father. She brought him so much happiness and then, when she was eighteen months old, he got pneumonia. I had a call at work to say he was sick, and twelve hours later he was dead.' She gave a little shrug. 'So, that was us, really.'

She blinked away the tears she always cried for Mick's wasted life and, lifting her head, she looked down into Sam's eyes. They were over-bright, and as she watched, a tear slid out of the corner of one and ran down into his hair. His hands gentle, he drew her down into his arms again and cradled her head against his chest.

'Molly, I'm so sorry. I had no idea. I wouldn't have asked.'

'It's a long time ago,' she said, but it didn't seem so long now, talking about it, and she felt the tears welling again for the tragic waste. She should have shared this joy with Mick, too, she thought. It was so unfair—so horribly, horribly unfair.

A sob rose in her throat, and Sam made a tutting noise and rocked her gently, like a child, while she wept for what the fates had taken away. Then she slept, and when she woke Sam was gone, and the sheets were cold.

She got up, sliding her legs over the edge of the bed and padding across the room. There was a robe on the back of the door, and she slipped it on and belted it tightly, then went looking for him.

Sam was gutted.

If he'd only known—if he'd had the slightest idea of how much she still loved Mick, he wouldn't have touched her. He couldn't have. That precious gift she'd given him last night had been Mick's, and Mick's alone, and he felt like a grave robber.

Oh, she'd participated willingly enough, but she was a young, healthy woman. Of course she'd been willing. It was biology, nothing more, and if he'd allowed himself to read anything more into it, well, this morning had certainly shown him the truth. He couldn't do it again. He'd been married to Crystal when she'd been in love with another man, and this was ten times worse. He couldn't compete with a ghost, and he had no intention of trying.

He felt a huge, raw pain inside, a pain like nothing he'd ever felt before, and he slipped quietly out of bed, amidst the burned-out candles and the bruised rose petals, and went downstairs, still naked.

He went into the shower off the utility room, closed the door and went into the cubicle, turning the water on full and standing motionless, head bowed, under the spray.

A sob fought its way free, and then another. Turning his face into the wall, he gave himself up to the pain.

Common sense resurrected itself before he drowned. He wasn't married to Molly, she didn't want that from him. She'd suggested an affair, and he'd taken her up on it. He was being stupid. Nothing had really changed, except his feelings.

OK, that was a pretty big nothing, but even so, he wasn't sure that a more permanent relationship between them would be a good idea. There were still all the complications of Jack.

'You're justifying it unnecessarily, Gregory,' he told himself angrily, slamming the lever down and cutting off the tepid water. 'It's an affair. You're both adults. So she's got baggage—so what? So have you. Just enjoy it while it lasts, and to hell with commitment.'

He towelled himself roughly dry, found some clothes in the tumble-dryer that would do, and started clearing up.

Molly found him in the kitchen, up to his elbows in suds, and she went up behind him and slipped her arms around his waist.

'You should have called me, I would have helped you,' she said.

He grunted, but he didn't speak. He didn't stop, either, just carried on washing the pans until he'd finished, then dried his hands and turned into her arms.

'You needed to sleep,' he said, but so much later she'd almost forgotten what she'd been talking about. 'Coffee or tea?'

'Oh, tea. I can't start the day with coffee.'

She perched on the edge of the table, her legs crossed, and watched him while he made it, wondering if she was imagining it or if he was in a strange mood. When he turned, mugs in hand, he gave her an odd, unreadable look and set the mugs down.

'Oh, Molly.'

He walked over to her, put his arms round her and cradled her against his chest.

She tipped her head back and looked up at him. 'Sam? What is it?'

'Nothing. It must be all those aphrodisiacs we had last night.'

His smile was faint and didn't reach his eyes, and she lifted a hand and cradled his cheek. It was rough with stubble, but he smelt of soap and his hair was damp.

'I need a shower,' she said. 'Come and help me.'

'I've showered.'

'But I haven't,' she said. Slipping off the edge of the table, she held out her hand. 'Show me where it is.'

'There's one here—it's got better water pressure than the one upstairs.'

'But is it near the bed?'

Sam's eyes darkened. 'No—but I'm sure we'll manage.'

He took her hand, and led her through into a bright little room, fully tiled and still steamy from his shower. He flipped the lever, stripped off his clothes and eased the dressing-gown from her shoulders. Then, closing the cubicle door behind them, he turned her away from him and soaped her thoroughly under the stinging spray.

Her thighs clenched on his hand, and she turned in his arms, her eyes searching his. There was nothing there but desire, hot and raw and hungry, and as the water pelted down on them, he lifted her and lowered her down onto him.

She gasped aloud, and his mouth found hers and he drove into her, again and again and again, until she felt the ripples start. She clung to him, her nails biting into the hot, slick flesh of his shoulders, striving…

'Sam?'

'Come for me, Molly,' he said roughly. 'Come for me…'

She felt herself fall apart, felt his response, instant and so powerful she was almost afraid, and then his voice, muffled by the water, saying her name in a rough, strained whisper that she could hardly hear.

Then something else that could have been 'I love you…'

CHAPTER TEN

MOLLY was puzzled.

She didn't know what had happened, but something had, and the more she thought about it that night, the more convinced she was that it was something to do with Mick. It had been fine until Sam had asked about him, and then it had all gone pear-shaped. Well, not pear-shaped, exactly, but different.

But why? Because she'd cried? Even with her lack of experience she realised it was pretty lousy etiquette to cry about another man all over the man you'd just made love with, but he'd asked her about Mick, and she'd just told him.

Too much detail? Too much everything, probably, and then crying about it had just been the finishing touch. Sam was probably sulking because he'd made so much effort and then she'd cried about someone else. To be fair, she might have sulked, too.

Oh, well, it was no use crying over spilt milk. She'd talk to him in the morning at work. In the meantime she needed to get some sleep before she went quite insane. She turned over, thumped the pillow again and closed her eyes.

Pointless.

She went downstairs and made herself a cup of tea, then took it into the sitting room and sat down on the sofa, right opposite the pictures of Mick. She studied them thoughtfully.

'I wonder what you'd make of him,' she asked him, but

there was no answer. There never was. She was truly on her own now, and after eight years she was pretty used to it. She looked at the photos again, photos of another Molly at another time, and thought that if it wasn't for Libby, she'd put them away. She didn't need them to remind her of Mick. She carried him in a special place in her heart and always would, but she'd moved on years ago.

Four years, to be exact—the time she'd met Sam.

Oh, Sam, she thought, and her throat clogged with tears. What have I said to hurt you? Something, but what? Is it just your ego?

There was no point in asking him, either. He wouldn't talk to her, any more than Mick used to. What was it about men that they couldn't talk about their feelings? Women did it all the time—and men committed most of the violent crimes in the world. Because of pent-up emotion?

Probably.

Molly put her empty mug back in the kitchen and went back to bed, finally falling asleep some time after two. She woke at seven, hustled Libby off to school and went to work. She was on a sensible shift today, office hours, and although it meant that Libby had to walk to her grandparents' after school, at least they didn't have such a revoltingly early start.

There was no sign of Sam, but she'd deal with him later. First of all, she needed to find out how Rosalind had got on over the weekend, and if she was going to keep her beautiful little daughter, and if her parents were able to support her through it.

She was sure they would, once they'd got over the shock of knowing that their granddaughter had been born in a cubicle in a public toilet.

She went down to the nursing station and was told that Rosalind and her baby were fine, and they'd gone home with her parents the day before, all rifts if not healed, at least on the way to it. Molly was sorry not to have seen her again, but at least the outcome was a happy one and the newshounds weren't still haunting the department.

She was called down to A and E during the course of the morning to attend to a woman who'd gone into labour following a fall. She was being stitched, and they wanted Molly's assessment of her labour to know whether they should keep her there a little longer or transfer her straight to Maternity.

The first person she saw as she went in was Nick Baker, and he greeted her with a warm if weary smile.

'Hello, Dad,' she said, and he chuckled.

'Hi. Come to see our pregnant lady?'

'I have. How are things at home?'

'Wonderful. Sally's shattered, but the baby's lovely. He's as good as gold. Thank you for putting up with us, by the way, and being so good to Sally.'

She laughed. 'My pleasure. I'll look forward to delivering the next one.'

'Oh, give us a little while to get over the shock,' he said with a rueful chuckle. 'Your lady's in here.'

He drew back the cubicle curtain. 'Ann, this is Molly. She's a midwife. She's come to have a look at you and see if you need to be transferred to Maternity or if we can finish you off first.'

The nurse who was stitching her arm snipped the suture and stepped back out of the way, and Molly gave her a fleeting smile and took her place beside their patient.

'Oh, dear, you have had a bit of a tumble, haven't you?' Molly said, looking at the cut. 'I'm just going to take a quick look at you, and see how your labour's coming on. Is this your first?'

'No—my third. I feel really odd, though. I didn't feel

like this with either of the others. I don't know if it was the fall, but I feel so breathless and dizzy, and I've got this abdominal pain now that just won't go away—it doesn't feel like a contraction.'

Molly didn't like the sound of that, and clearly neither did Nick.

'That's a change from a few minutes ago. I think we could ask Sam to come down and take a look, and I'll rustle up a consent form,' he said.

While he was doing that, Molly kept a close eye on Ann's blood pressure and respiration rate, as well as the foetal heart rate.

It wasn't a good picture. Her blood pressure was falling, her resps were going up, and the baby's heart was slowing. On top of that her abdomen was rigid. It was looking more and more like a placental abruption, and Molly wanted Sam there fast. 'I think we need to get some fluids into you,' she said, and put a large-bore cannula in her hand in readiness.

She was about to find out what had happened to Sam when he appeared round the curtain, and her heart thumped. 'This is Ann,' she said, and quickly filled him in.

He didn't hesitate. 'Get some plasma expander into her, stat, Molly, please,' he murmured, and then, laying one hand on Ann's rigid abdomen, he took her uninjured hand in the other and explained the situation.

'Ann, I'm sorry, we're going to have to take you up to Theatre and deliver your baby by Caesarian section. Your placenta may be coming away, and we have to move fairly quickly.'

Fairly quickly? Molly all but ran to keep up with him as he strode along the corridor to the lift, the bag of plasma expander held aloft and the consent form lying unsigned as yet on Ann's chest. She went up to Theatre with them, leaving them at the door and going back down to the ward with a heavy heart.

Sam hadn't even glanced at her, except to find out information about their patient. OK, it had been fraught, but it had been fraught before and he'd always found time for a smile. So, was she just imagining it, or had she really upset him?

Unless it was nothing to do with Mick and she'd just put two and two together and made five. Maybe he was just bored with her—he'd got what he wanted, and now he'd lost interest.

No. She didn't want to think that, it was too painful, even though she acknowledged that it was quite likely to be true. After all, a man with the skill and expertise to set up a seduction scene like that wasn't likely to be satisfied for long with a fumbling novice, was he?

Especially if he was still in love with his wife. Maybe her talk of Mick had brought back memories of Crystal, and although her behaviour had been less than perfect, perhaps he still loved her anyway.

Love was a funny thing, there was no accounting for it.

She resolved to talk to Sam the first chance she could find, and then lost herself in her work.

Sam opened Ann up, removed the baby and handed him to Josh Lancaster who was standing by to resuscitate him, then removed the placenta manually. The uterus contracted, the bleeding slowed and then stopped, and he heaved a sigh of relief.

That had been close—too close for comfort, he thought, finally hearing the baby cry.

'How is he?' he asked, and Josh shrugged.

'Not great. He's coming up, though. He's a few weeks early—have we got a gestation?'

'Not that I know of. They might have something in her notes.'

'Hmm.' Josh continued working on the baby while Sam tidied up the mother and closed, and then she went through to Recovery and Sam watched Josh as he worked.

'Were we too slow?'

Again, Josh shrugged. 'Hard to tell. I hope not. He'll need to be in SCBU for a few days, though, I think, at the very least. How's Mum?'

'OK. She'll need transfusing, but she'll be fine. I think it was just the fall. There was a lot of bruising on the abdominal wall over the placental site, but I had a look round and couldn't see any other damage. There didn't seem to be any other bleeding, anyway. Is there any evidence of trauma on the baby?'

'No—just the anoxia. He's responding, I'm pretty confident now that he'll be all right.'

Sam nodded. 'I'll go and tell his mother, and get her admitted to the ward. I'll see you. Thanks, Josh.'

He went down to the ward, but Molly was busy, and he wasn't sure he wanted to see her anyway. It was too difficult at work, and he was beginning to think the whole thing had been a lousy idea. Maybe he'd give them both time to cool off.

It was two days before Molly saw Sam, and she got the feeling he was avoiding her again. This time, though, when she managed to corner him in the canteen, she didn't beat about the bush.

'Sam, what's going on?' she asked quietly but firmly. 'Last weekend you couldn't seem to get enough of me. Now you won't talk to me. I want to know why.'

He shook his head. 'I'm sorry, I owe you an apology. I've been really busy at home. I've been decorating in the evenings, and I've had a lot to do here.'

'That much?' she said sceptically. 'So much that you didn't have time even for a quiet hello?'

He sighed and rammed his hand through his hair. 'It's not that I won't talk to you, Molly. I just haven't had time, and I don't think we should seek each other out at work. It isn't good for our professional relationship.'

She laughed a little bitterly. 'That didn't seem to trouble you on Saturday when you were kissing me in the ward kitchen,' she said in an undertone.

'Saturday was different.'

'You're telling me. And now you've got me out of your system.'

He shook his head. 'Molly, that's not it. I haven't had time for anyone, it isn't personal—'

'Well, it damned well was at the weekend!' she said shortly. 'It's all right, Sam. I'm a big girl, I can take it. I threw myself at you. Only a fool would have turned me down, and you were never that.'

'Molly, stop it,' he said impatiently. 'I really have been busy.'

'So when are you free?'

He hesitated for a moment, then sighed. 'Tonight? Can you get a babysitter?'

'Libby's at her grandparents' until seven. I'll cook you supper, if you can get away.'

'I'll do my best.'

She stood up. 'You do that. And in the meantime, I'd like to make arrangements to see Jack again at the weekends.'

'Of course. Tell me when, and I'll see what I can do.'

Sam got to his feet, and for the briefest moment their

eyes met. She could have sworn she saw pain in their cobalt depths, but then that blank look was back, and he walked away, leaving her standing, shaking, in the middle of the canteen.

'Molly? Are you OK?'

She looked round blindly, and saw Nick Baker coming towards her, concern etched onto his handsome features.

'I'm fine,' she lied. 'How are you all?'

'Oh—great. How's Ann?'

'Ann?'

'The lady with the antepartum haemorrhage.'

'Oh. She's fine. The baby's OK. Sam got her in the nick of time.' Her voice trembled on his name, and she rammed her hands in her pockets and stepped back. 'Well, if you'll excuse me, I have to go. Patients to see.'

She turned and walked away, resisting the urge to run. She wanted time to herself, to think through her conversation with Sam and work out what she was going to say to him tonight, but she didn't get a chance. The rest of the day was chaotic, and she rushed home, threw together a risotto and bathed in no time flat.

And then the phone rang. It was Sam.

'Molly, I'm sorry, I won't be able to make it. Something's come up at work and I won't get away until much later.'

'So come later.'

'I can't. I'm sorry. I'll see you tomorrow.'

She cradled the phone, stared at it for a moment and then rang Angie.

She didn't beat about the bush. 'Is there a difference,' she asked bluntly, 'between making love and sex?'

There was a moment of startled silence, then Angie said cautiously, 'I don't know. Yes, I think so. Molly, what happened?'

She gave a hollow laugh. 'I don't know. On Saturday night we made love—quite definitely. On Sunday morning—it felt different. Colder. More desperate. I don't know.'

'Desperate? That's an odd word to use.'

Molly sighed. 'I think I hurt him. He asked about Mick, and…'

'And?' Angie prompted.

'I cried. I told him things I've never told a soul, and then I cried.'

'Oh, Molly. Have you talked to him?'

She shook her head, then remembered she was on the phone and Angie couldn't see her. 'No. I can't. He won't talk to me.'

'Oh, men. Couldn't you shoot them? Look, Molly, you have to talk to him—if you want to sort it out, that is. I take it you do.'

'Oh, lord, yes. Angie, I love him. I thought I loved him before the weekend, but now…'

Her control shattered, and the strain of the last few days caught up with her. 'I'm sorry. I have to go,' she said, and hung up, tears pouring down her cheeks. She needed him, and because she'd pushed it, moved their relationship onto a different level, she'd lost him.

Well, she thought she'd lost him. From where she was standing, it certainly felt like it, and the pain was unbearable.

When she'd recovered enough to speak, she phoned her in-laws and asked them if they could keep Libby for the night. 'Something's come up,' she said. 'I have to work late.'

'Sure. We'll take her to school. Is everything OK?'

'Yes,' she lied. 'I'll see you tomorrow. Thank you for your help.'

'Any time. Looking after her's a pleasure. She's all we have of Mick, don't forget that.'

As if she could. Molly hung up, took the risotto out of the oven and went upstairs, holding a cold flannel over her face to soothe her red-rimmed eyes.

Pointless. It would take more than a cold flannel when she kept aggravating them again with another bout of tears.

'You're a fool,' she told her blotchy reflection. 'Go and eat that risotto, see if there's anything on television, and then get an early night.'

She didn't bother to get dressed. What was the point? Sam wasn't coming. She'd stay in her comfy, ratty old dressing-gown and slum it.

Sam felt like a heel.

He'd hurt Molly, he knew that, but he couldn't talk about it. What could he say? 'You're in love with a dead man, and I can't deal with it'? Hardly.

Debbie, of course, didn't beat about the bush. He thought he'd scoured all trace of Molly from the house, but she found the condom packet on the floor in his bedroom and put it back conspicuously on his bedside table.

'Things looking up, then?' she asked, and he grunted. 'I just wondered—what with the condoms appearing over the weekend.'

'Mind your own damn business,' he growled, and she blinked and stared at him.

'Oops. Didn't it go well?'

He laughed without humour. 'Not exactly. Put it like this—I'm not in the market for competing with her dead husband. I've already played second fiddle once. I'm not doing it again, and certainly not to a ghost.'

'Second fiddle? Are you kidding? The way she looks at you?'

'It's just sex, Debbie, believe me,' he said bluntly. Was he hoping to shock her into leaving it alone? If so, he'd reckoned without her Cockney grit.

'You're nuts. Did you blow it or what?'

'No, I didn't blow it,' he said emphatically. 'Debbie, leave it. She's coming over some time to see Jack, and I won't be here. Could I leave him with you to deal with it?'

She eyed him steadily. 'Have you told her how you feel?'

'There's nothing to tell her, Debbie. It's irrelevant. It isn't that sort of relationship.'

He left the room, Debbie's snort of derision ringing in his ears, and plunged himself into a needless reorganisation of his computer files. Anything rather than think about Molly sitting on the kitchen table in his dressing-gown, with her legs showing where the fabric had parted, and the shadow of her breasts visible in the deep, gaping V of the neck...

Or then there was the sitting room, where they'd danced together, or the dining room, scene of the greatest seduction of all time—and he couldn't even go in his bedroom. He avoided it until late at night, and went in there in the dark with the benefit of a few glasses of wine to knock him out.

It didn't work, though. Nothing worked, and he wondered if playing second fiddle would actually, in the long run, be worse than playing nothing at all.

He looked at his watch. Eight-thirty. Libby would be in bed. He could go and talk to Molly, apologise for being such a bastard. After all, it was hardly her fault that she was still in love with Mick!

He grabbed his jacket, tapped on the communicating door and told Debbie that he was nipping out.

'Finally,' she said, and he closed the door with a defiant click and let himself out. He changed his mind about a hundred times on the short drive over there, and when he arrived, he hesitated on the road outside until someone wanted to come out of their drive and he had to move.

'Oh, hell,' he muttered. Turning into her drive, he cut the engine and strode to the door without any further prevarication. He leant on the frame, his finger poised on the bellpush, but before he could press it the door swung open and Molly stood there in a disreputable old dressing-gown with a wary look on her face that made him feel a complete rat.

'You said come later. Am I too late?'

Her smile was faint, and just made him feel worse.

'Of course not. Libby's not here, she's staying with her grandparents. Come in.'

Sam stepped over the threshold, closed the door behind himself and drew her into his arms with a ragged sigh. 'I'm sorry, Molly,' he said gruffly. 'I haven't been very good to you this week.'

'No, I'm sorry. I shouldn't have gone on about Mick.'

'Forget it. I don't want to talk about it.'

He threaded his fingers through her hair, lowered his mouth to hers and kissed her tenderly. 'Forgive me,' he murmured against her lips, and with a little sigh she moved closer into his arms.

'There's nothing to forgive,' she said, and eased away, looking up at him. 'Have you eaten? There's some risotto left.'

He shook his head. He hadn't eaten, but he didn't feel hungry. Not for food, anyway. He kissed her again, and she melted against him for a moment, then drawing away she held out her hand.

'Come on,' she said softly. He placed his hand in hers

and she led him upstairs to her bedroom, closed the door and turned to him. The bedside light was on, casting a soft glow over the room, and she slipped off the dressing-gown and reached up for him, pushing his jacket off his shoulders, stripping off his sweater, unfastening the stud on his jeans and sliding down the zip, her fingers so near to him he could feel the fire.

They closed round him and he groaned and took her mouth, cupping her bottom in his hands and rocking her against him.

So it was just sex for her. So what? Suddenly it didn't feel so bad...

Molly saw Jack at the weekends, but Sam wasn't there.

'He had to go out,' Debbie said the third time it happened, but something about the way she said it made Molly wonder. He was still being a little distant at work, and the only time she got anywhere near him was when they made love.

Or had sex, or whatever he wanted to call it. At that time, he let down his guard, and for a few brief moments she had the real Sam, the Sam she loved from the bottom of her heart.

Still, she put the thought aside and concentrated on Jack, and it was a bitter-sweet experience. He was mangling some play-dough in the corner of the kitchen at his little table, and she was sitting at the big table, watching him. He was a lovely child, just like a miniature of his father to look at, and every bit as stubborn. She wondered—

'Tea?'

She shook her head. 'No, thanks, Debbie. I'm—not drinking tea at the moment,' she said, avoiding the woman's eye, but she may as well not have bothered.

'If you're not drinking tea for the same reason I'm not

drinking tea, then you've got to tell Sam,' she said in a low voice.

Her eyes flew to Debbie's, startled, then she looked away, colour running over her skin. 'How?'

'I don't know. When you've worked it out, you can tell me. I daren't tell Mark, he's under so much pressure at the moment. He's trying to set up this business, and the last thing he needs is me losing this job because of that.'

'Would you? Surely not. You can look after Jack and a baby. Women do that all the time—it's what we do best.'

'My baby, or yours?' Debbie said drily, and got up to put the kettle on. 'Herbal tea?'

Molly laughed wryly. 'Please. And then go and tell Mark.'

'He'll just worry.'

'I'll talk to Sam for you.'

Debbie shook her head. 'No. I'll do it. You talk to him about you, because you look like hell, you know, and so does he.' She sat down again, eyeing Molly thoughtfully. 'Can I ask you something really personal? Are you still in love with your husband?'

'Mick? No, of course not. I mean, I treasure his memory, but—Debbie, I've been in love with Sam for years, ever since we first met and talked about me having a baby for them.'

Debbie nodded. 'I thought he was talking bull. He told me to butt out.'

Molly laughed, then thought about Debbie's words for a moment and froze. 'Hang on. Does he think I'm still in love with Mick?'

Debbie nodded again. 'Yeah. Talked a lot of rubbish about second fiddle.'

'What?' Molly was stunned, but, thinking about it, it all made perfect sense. It had been after she'd told him about

Mick that it had all gone wrong, and she'd sensed it was something to do with him, but that? Never. 'He's crazy.'

'So tell him yourself. Maybe he'll believe you. He'll be back in an hour. What about Libby? Do you need to get back for her?'

Molly shook her head. 'No, she's gone to a sleepover party.'

'Right. We'll take Jack, and you can have the house to yourselves. We'll give you till nine tonight. If you need longer, ring my mobile. The number's in the phone, it's memory two.'

Molly nodded, then swallowed hard. Make or break, she thought, this was it. By the end of the evening she intended to have this sorted out, or she was leaving.

Baby or no baby.

Sam turned into his drive and stopped dead. Molly's car was there, and the lights were on, but there was no sign of Debbie and Mark and he wondered what was wrong.

Jack, he thought, fear clawing at his throat. He'd left his mobile behind by accident—had they been trying to contact him?

He let himself in and strode through to the kitchen, to find Molly sitting there at the table, her hands folded in her lap, her face pale.

'What is it? What's wrong with Jack?'

'Nothing's wrong with Jack.'

'Mark, then.'

'Nothing. There's nothing wrong with anyone—only us. Debbie and Mark have taken Jack out so we can talk.'

Her words registered slowly, and he hooked out a chair and sat down opposite her, relief wiping the strength from his legs. Then the relief faded, replaced by a sickening dread.

She was going to tell him to go to hell. He deserved it, the way he'd treated her for the past three weeks, but he couldn't seem to help himself.

'Can you just do one thing for me?' she asked him, the apparent calm of her voice betrayed by a slight tremor. 'If I ask you a question, will you answer it honestly? And I'll do the same.'

Sam hesitated for so long she thought she'd lost him, then he inclined his head a fraction.

'If I can,' he said.

Well, that was a start, she supposed.

'Do you want to go first?'

Again he hesitated, then he shook his head. 'No. You go first.'

Molly took a deep breath, then plunged in, her heart hammering.

'What do you want most in the world, Sam?'

His head came up, his eyes locking with hers, and this time she knew she hadn't imagined the pain in them.

'You,' he said unevenly, 'but I don't know if I'm strong enough to live in Mick's shadow. He was obviously a hell of a man, and I had no right to ask you about him that night. It made me feel...' He broke off, shaking his head and searching for words. 'As if I'd intruded in something I had no right to. That night belonged to you two, Molly. It should have been yours. I had no right to touch you.'

'Sam, that's nonsense. I wanted you, and you gave me a wonderful night—a night to remember. It was everything I'd wanted, for four long years.'

'Four?'

She nodded. 'Four. Since I met you. There is no shadow from Mick, Sam. He's gone, and I accepted that ages ago. I've loved you for years, ever since our first meeting.

That's why I agreed to have a child for you, because I wanted to carry your child inside me—because I loved you.'

His eyes closed fleetingly, and when he opened them his lashes were clumped with tears. 'Oh, God, Molly. I wanted to share it—to touch you, to hold you, to feel my baby kick against my side at night—but I couldn't. You weren't mine to touch, and I needed you. When he was born, I wanted to take you home with me. I wanted to watch you suckle him, but it just couldn't happen. That's one of my greatest regrets, amongst many, that you never suckled him.'

'I did,' she confessed. 'I know Crystal didn't want me to, but that night he cried, and I went to him in the nursery, and I fed him. It was the last thing I could give him.'

She closed her eyes, hot tears spilling down her cheeks, and then she was in his arms, gathered up against his chest as he carried her through to the study and sat down with her cradled on his lap.

'I love you,' he said unsteadily. 'Oh, God, Molly, I love you.'

His mouth found hers, his kisses tender, cherishing, almost reverent. He kissed away her tears, then rocked her gently against his chest.

'Can I ask you something?'

She nodded. 'If you promise to talk about my answer.'

His smile was crooked and a little strained. 'I'm sorry.'

'Don't be. What was it?'

'What do you want most in the world?'

'Apart from you? For us to be a family.'

His arms tightened convulsively. 'Oh, thank God. And maybe, when we've been married for a while—you will marry me, won't you?' he asked, breaking off to look down at her, sudden uncertainty in his eyes.

She smiled, her hand coming up to cup his rough jaw, reassuring him. 'Of course I'll marry you.'

'And then, after a while, how would you feel about having another child?'

'Wonderful. I'm glad you brought that up.' She laughed softly. 'Because a little under eight months should do it.'

'Eight...?' He lifted his head and stared down at her, puzzlement giving way to pure, unadulterated joy. 'Oh, Molly...' His hand slipped between them, coming to rest over their child. 'Are you sure?'

'I've done it before, I recognise the symptoms. And anyway, there was this little blue line on the test—'

'But you're on the Pill.'

'I had that bug—I didn't even think about it. I'm a bit of a novice like that.'

'Thank goodness.' Sam's hand splayed over the baby, and his eyes settled on the flat plane of her abdomen. 'We're going to have a baby,' he said incredulously. 'A real baby—our baby, yours and mine. Oh, Molly, I can't believe it.'

His arms tightened round her, and his lips found hers and brushed them tenderly. 'It's crazy but I always felt that Jack was your son, that you were his mother, and having you back in our lives somehow seems so right, but to go through the pregnancy and the birth with you, knowing we'll be together afterwards—you can have no idea how I've longed for that.'

'Me, too,' she said, resting her face against his shoulder, drawing comfort from his warmth. 'To have a baby, knowing I won't have to give it away at the end, will just be bliss, and to be back in Jack's life... I've worried so much about Jack—he will be all right with this, won't he?'

Sam nodded. 'Oh, yes. He's said the odd thing about some of the pregnant mums at nursery—like, could we have a mummy and a new baby, too, for instance. Throw a big sister into the equation as well, and he'll be delirious.' He chuckled, then looked down into her eyes again, that gentle concern back. 'How about Libby? Will she be all right about it?'

'She'll be ecstatic. She's always wanted a little brother or sister, and now she'll have two. And a father. She's missed having a father.'

Sam's face clouded. 'I'm not Mick, Molly.'

'I know. I don't want you to be. I want you to be yourself—stubborn, awkward, close-mouthed—'

'That's changing, I promise. I'll talk to you whenever things feel wrong. I've lost one marriage because I had no idea of my wife's feelings. I don't intend to do it again.'

She kissed him. 'Good. We won't have to fight about it.' She kissed him again, and again, and then glanced at her watch. 'We've got two hours before Debbie and Mark get back. Got any ideas?'

His smile was slow and lazy and worth waiting for. 'The kitchen table,' he murmured. And standing up, he carried her down the hall…

EPILOGUE

IT WAS a glorious September day, the first anniversary of their first night together, and they were all gathered in the garden at the cottage for the baby's christening.

Debbie was running round waiting on people in a—for her—demure cerise T-shirt dress that almost matched her hair, and Mark was propped against the apple tree, their six-month-old son Jordan squirming in his arms and threatening to dislodge the ring in his eyebrow.

Their business was flourishing, and between them and Molly, they were caring for all the children on alternate days. A bit of a nightmare in the holidays, but Molly was only going to be working two days a week, and Debbie was around to help on the other three as well, and so far it seemed to be going fine.

Sam ran his eye over the rest of their friends: Angie and Doug, the baby's godparents, with little Laura, Molly's first surrogate baby; Lyn, Molly's friend from her surrogacy support group, with her new partner; Nick and Sally Baker, with one-year-old Joshua; Sue, one of Molly's colleagues, with her husband and child; and, of course, all the grandparents—including the Hammonds and, unbelievably, Crystal's parents, who'd asked humbly if they could share in the celebrations.

The children were having fun—Libby and Jack and the others—giggling and chasing each other round the apple tree, their faces glowing with health and happiness and mischief. Sam smiled indulgently, and looked down at the baby in Molly's arms, a lump in his throat.

They'd called her Bonnie, and she was well named. She was perfect—a miniature Jack, but with something of Libby about her, too, and Molly was the picture of contentment. She was feeding Bonnie now, the baby's pink rosebud mouth fastened on her nipple and suckling hungrily, her fingers tiny and creased against the blue-veined smoothness of Molly's breast.

Her little eyes drooped shut, and her mouth stopped working as she slid into sleep.

'I'll take her,' Sam murmured, and lifted her from Molly's arms to cradle her against his shoulder. Their eyes met, and he smiled, a great tenderness welling inside him. 'All right?'

'Never better. The perfect end to a perfect year.'

He bent and kissed her, just the lightest touch of his lips to hers, a promise—and a thank you for a future he'd never thought he'd have.

A mother for his son, a child of their own, a beautiful stepdaughter—and the woman dearest to his heart to walk by his side every day for the rest of his life.

As she'd said, the perfect end to a perfect year...

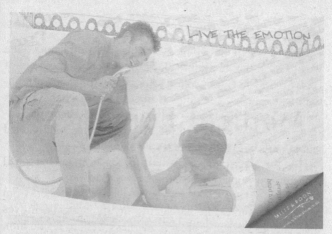

Modern Romance™
...seduction and
passion guaranteed

Tender Romance™
...love affairs that
last a lifetime

Medical Romance™
...medical drama
on the pulse

Historical Romance™
...rich, vivid and
passionate

Sensual Romance™
...sassy, sexy and
seductive

Blaze Romance™
...the temperature's
rising

27 new titles every month.

Live the emotion

MILLS & BOON®

MB3

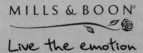

MILLS & BOON

Live the emotion

Medical Romance™

OUTBACK ENGAGEMENT *by Meredith Webber*

Outback vet Tom Fleming has a problem. After featuring in a magazine as the 'Lonely Country Bachelor' he is surrounded by would-be wives! Merriwee's new doctor, Anna Talbot, is beautiful, blonde and engaged. Perhaps Tom should claim that *he* gave her the ring – having a fake fiancée may end all his woman troubles...

THE PLAYBOY CONSULTANT *by Maggie Kingsley*

Surgeon David Hart puts commitment into work rather than relationships. So he's surprised by his turn-about in feelings when his senior registrar turns out to be Dr Rachel Dunwoody, the woman who walked out on him six years ago! David has some urgent questions. Why did she leave? And, most urgently, how can he get her back?

THE BABY EMERGENCY *by Carol Marinelli*

When Shelly Weaver returned to the children's ward as a single mum, she discovered it was Dr Ross Bodey's first night back too. On discovering her newly single status he'd come back – for her! Suddenly Ross was asking her to change her life for ever – yet Shelly had her son to consider now. Could she make room for them both in her life?

On sale 7th November 2003

Available at most branches of WHSmith, Tesco, Martins, Borders, Eason, Sainsbury's and all good paperback bookshops.

1003/03a

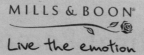

4 FREE

books and a surprise gift!

We would like to take this opportunity to thank you for reading this Mills & Boon® book by offering you the chance to take FOUR more specially selected titles from the Medical Romance™ series absolutely FREE! We're also making this offer to introduce you to the benefits of the Reader Service™—

★ FREE home delivery
★ FREE gifts and competitions
★ FREE monthly Newsletter
★ Exclusive Reader Service discount
★ Books available before they're in the shops

Accepting these FREE books and gift places you under no obligation to buy, you may cancel at any time, even after receiving your free shipment. Simply complete your details below and return the entire page to the address below. *You don't even need a stamp!*

YES! Please send me 4 free Medical Romance books and a surprise gift. I understand that unless you hear from me, I will receive 6 superb new titles every month for just £2.60 each, postage and packing free. I am under no obligation to purchase any books and may cancel my subscription at any time. The free books and gift will be mine to keep in any case.

M3ZEE

Ms/Mrs/Miss/Mr ....Initials.............................
<small>BLOCK CAPITALS PLEASE</small>

Surname ....

Address ....

....

....Postcode..........................

Send this whole page to:
UK: FREEPOST CN81, Croydon, CR9 3WZ
EIRE: PO Box 4546, Kilcock, County Kildare (stamp required)